# ANOTHER SHOT

D1419399

# ANOTHER SHOT

**STEPHEN ANTHONY BROTHERTON**

The Book Guild Ltd

First published in Great Britain in 2017 by
The Book Guild Ltd
9 Priory Business Park
Wistow Road, Kibworth
Leicestershire, LE8 0RX
Freephone: 0800 999 2982
www.bookguild.co.uk
Email: info@bookguild.co.uk
Twitter: @bookguild

Typeset in Minion Pro

Printed and bound in Great Britain by CPI Group (UK) Ltd, Croydon, CR0 4YY


ISBN 978 1912083 107


British Library Cataloguing in Publication Data.
A catalogue record for this book is available from the British Library.

*Iris May Brotherton: 'You deserve another shot at life, Mom.'*

*Freddie – July 2015*

The jangling brass doorway bell heralded my arrival at the coffee shop. Several of the regulars looked up, but they quickly returned to their gossipy chatter about families, friends and neighbours, hushed voices back-dropped by the sound of a gushing steamer, grinding beans and clattering crockery.

'Skimmed milk latte,' said the waitress, already pouring the red top milk into the jug.

It used to make me feel special, the fact that they knew me, knew what I wanted, but it had soured with repetition. I'd become my drink order – that's what it felt like. But it was okay. People-watching in this place made me feel part of the world, got me away from the house for a few hours.

And it was here she came back to me.

I hadn't seen her for three decades and suddenly there she was, standing next to my table.

'Hello, Freddie.'

*Freddie – November 1979*

She walked across Max's nightclub dance floor towards me as Blondie's 'Dreaming' started up.

'I thought you'd never ask,' she said.

I wouldn't. What would have been the point? She was first division and I was Sunday pub league. I stood in silence, mouth open, waiting for the punchline, waiting for my mate, Jack, to burst out laughing. Piss-take of the century.

'I'll take that as a no then,' she said, turning to walk away, jolting me back to my senses.

'Wait. Dance. Yes.'

Monosyllabic, but at least I'd found my voice.

*Freddie – July 2015*

It felt like I'd messed up the coffee shop reunion by breaking my five-second hug rule and clinging on for too long. I remembered a time when holding each other for all eternity wouldn't have been enough.

I scooped up the newspapers from the second seat and dropped them to the floor.

'Sit down,' I said. 'I can't believe it's you.'

'You're looking well, Freddie,' she said.

'And you. It's been a long time.'

An awkward silence fell as we met each other's eyes – her line of nose freckles reminding me of the mole above her belly button and triggering an age-old desire to join the dots. I could feel the regulars staring, trying to work out who the stranger was. She looked nervously around the room, china cats and dogs staring down at her from a Welsh dresser.

'What are you doing here, Jo-Jo?'

She reached across the table and squeezed my hand.

'I'm looking for you,' she said.

*Freddie – November 1979*

We didn't dance to Blondie. I spent most of the record explaining why it wasn't a good idea for a gangly man to do disco dancing. I expected her to get bored, to walk away, but she stayed and nodded, looking up at me as though I was explaining the theory of DNA.

'I'm Jo-Jo,' she said.

'Right,' I said. 'Jo-Jo. Freddie. I mean, that's me. My name's Freddie.'

Dr Hook came to my rescue. 'More Like the Movies'.

'I can do this one,' I said.

We walked hand in hand onto the dance floor.

For the next three and a half minutes I was more conscious of my body's proximity to another human being than I'd ever been before in my life. I had this voice inside my head reminding me of my rules – 'Don't hold her too close'; 'Keep your hand flat in the middle of her back'; 'Don't tread on her feet'; 'Don't sing'. I relaxed, closed my eyes, went with the sway from side to side, opened my eyes, smiled at her, she was real, she smiled back. And then – I could have kissed him – the DJ played the Commodores, 'Still', followed by Exile's, 'Kiss You All Over'. Three in a row. Ten glorious minutes of holding her as close as I dared, intoxicated by her white musk perfume. The lights came on. We handed in our tickets and collected our coats. I waved goodbye to Jack, left him searching for his sister, and offered to walk Jo-Jo home.

'Where do you live, Freddie?'

'Lower Farm,' I said.

'But that's in the opposite direction.'

I shrugged and she laughed. I'd never made anyone like her laugh before.

We crunched through the icy night. I was wearing my cousin's blue cord jacket and a pair of Pod shoes that had cost me most of a week's pay packet. I was distracted by the shoes, hoping the snow wasn't shredding them to pieces. She asked what I did. I told her I was on a YOP scheme, working at a timber yard. She told me she worked at a hairdresser's as a Saturday girl.

We reached a patch of green in the middle of a council estate, a big oak tree growing in its centre. She stopped walking. 'That's my house there,' she said.

She looked at me, her lips glistening with what I hoped was

strawberry lip gloss. I wanted to kiss her, but I froze. After a few seconds she smiled and touched my cheek. 'You're sweet,' she said. 'I'll call you.'

She reached her front door and waved.

I turned up my coat collar and headed home.


*Freddie – July 2015*

---

'Morning.'

Tom Stone, retired headmaster, unelected leader of the coffee-shop brigade, had sidled up to the table and was looking at me, waiting for his formal introduction.

'Tom,' I said. 'This is…'

'I'm an old friend,' said Jo-Jo, giving him a hard stare.

He looked at her, the smile disappearing from his face.

'Perhaps we can talk later,' I said. 'We're just in the middle of something.'

'Of course. I can see you're busy.'

He leaned lightly on his walking stick and limped back to his table. He sat down, shook his head and said something to his wife. They both looked over.

'Nosy old sods,' said Jo-Jo, still holding my hand.

'They're okay,' I said.

'You're too soft, Freddie. You always were.'

'Jo-Jo, it's been over thirty years. Why are you looking for me now?'

'Because it's the right time.'

'The right time for what?'

She hesitated, reached inside her coat pocket, which she'd draped over the back of her chair, and pulled out a black and white passport sized photograph.

'To give you this,' she said.

4

On the walk home from the nightclub, I reasoned through what had happened. She'd fancied a change from her 'Saturday Night Fever' blokes, I'd caught her eye and half an hour later she'd regretted it. She wouldn't call. Why would she?

Two days later, she called.

'Hi, it's me.'

For some bizarre reason, and I blame the Steve McQueen film on telly that night, I decided to play it cool. 'Hello, me,' I said.

She went quiet for a few seconds. 'Is that you, Freddie?'

'Sure is.'

'It's Jo-Jo.'

The stutter of insecurity in her voice shifted my brain into gear.

'Jo-Jo,' I said. 'I didn't think you'd call.'

'I nearly hung up. Perhaps I shouldn't have called.'

'I was hoping you'd call. I enjoyed our dance.'

'Me too.'

'It was bloody freezing walking home though.'

'I told you not to walk me back.'

'I'll wear my thermals next time.'

She laughed.

'So you work on a Saturday,' I said.

'Yeah, but I can't wait to leave that cow at the hairdressers. What about you?'

'Me?'

'Yeah. How's things with you? What have you been up to?'

I could have told her about spending the previous evening with Jack, sorting out my postcard collection of World War Two fighter planes. I had them in date order of manufacture and we'd reordered them into number of missions flown in combat.

'Oh, nothing much.' I said. 'Same old stuff.'

Silence.

'Do you fancy meeting up?' I said.


*Freddie – July 2015*

---

I could feel Tom and his wife still looking at us as I took the photograph from Jo-Jo.

'Do you remember where that was taken?' she said.

'Blackpool,' I said. 'God, we were so young.'

'Look at your hair. It's on your shoulders. You'd just bought that car.'

I studied the picture, resurfacing the memory of how she'd smartened me up in a black pork pie hat, Chelsea boots and hugging trousers she'd tapered herself. She was wearing a red beret, a pink cheesecloth shirt and a mod jacket with the collar turned up. She'd bought the beret from one of the market stalls in town, said it made her look like Marianne Faithfull.

'It's wonderful,' I said. 'But you haven't come all this way to bring me a photograph.'


*Freddie – May 1980*

---

I turned into Jo-Jo's street and dropped the speed of my second hand Chrysler Avenger down to twenty miles per hour, a Springsteen cassette on cue to provide the backing track for our first weekend away together. We'd spent the previous evening in Jo-Jo's bedroom plotting every detail. 'Isn't this a bit obsessive, Freddie,' she'd said, looking at my list. 'Do we really need to know where we're eating every meal?'

I pulled up outside her house and beeped the horn. Her face appeared briefly at the lounge window and then she was coming through the front door, clutching a tweed carpet bag. She threw the bag on the backseat and jumped in the passenger side.

'You got it. I can't believe you bought it.'

'Thank my mum. She lent me the money.'

'I'd rather thank you,' she said, dropping her arms around my neck and kissing me full on the lips.

I eased her gently away. 'Shall we go?' I said.

'Ready when you are. Turn the music up and get us there as fast as you can.'

I slammed the car into gear and screeched away from the kerb. Jo-Jo fell back in the passenger seat laughing, her loose auburn hair flinging itself around her tanned face. 'Easy tiger,' she said, putting her hand on my thigh. 'I would like to get there in one piece.'

I grinned and pushed in the tape. 'Growin Up' brought the stereo to life.

*Freddie – July 2015*

The brass bell jangled. We both looked over at the shop doorway. It was Dora, another of the regulars. She was clutching her Toy Poodle, Alfie.

'You'll have to keep him on your lap,' said the waitress.

'I know,' said Dora.

Jo-Jo took a sip of her coffee. 'There is something else, Freddie.'

I felt a rising panic in my stomach. 'What?' I said.

'I'm emigrating,' she said, gently placing her coffee cup back in its saucer. 'My husband, Jason, died last year and I'm off to join my daughter, Amy, in New Zealand. She's got two kids. Can you imagine me a granny? It's ridiculous.'

Husband. Daughter. She'd had a life – a life without me. 'I'll miss you,' I said.

She looked at me quizzically. 'We haven't seen each other for years.'

I felt the blood rush to my cheeks, conscious of having said something really stupid. 'Another country seems different,' I said. 'And it's so far away.'

'I know what you mean,' she said. 'I'm still getting used to the idea. It's all happened so quickly.'

'And you came to tell me? After all this time.'

'It sounds silly, but I didn't want to go without seeing you again.'

'How did you know I'd be here?'

'That mate of yours, Jack. We got chatting at a dementia charity event. His name jumped out from the delegate list.'

I smiled. Jo-Jo laughed.

'Poor Jack,' I said. 'He was really pissed off when that film came out. Threatened to sue Johnny Depp.'

'He was loving it at the conference. Had a big name badge with 'Jack Sparrow' emblazoned across his chest. You two stayed in touch then?'

'Yep. Don't know what I'd do without him. He's as straight as they come.'

'Not that straight,' she said.

'You worked that one out then.'

'First thing he said to me. "You've probably heard I'm queer, darling." I thought he was winding me up.'

'That's Jack,' I said. 'Says it as it is.'

She was looking at me, stroking my hand. I wanted her to say something, anything.

'It's strange to think of you married,' I said.

It was too hot to run but that hadn't stopped us tying our hair in pony-tails, putting on matching trainers, track suit bottoms and tee-shirts, all found by Jo-Jo on our last shopping trip to town, and setting off on what had become our regular Sunday morning jog down the lane; past Sam the gypsy and his greyhounds, all sitting outside his battered and rusty caravan, and then back along the side of the canal. Twenty minutes in, we reached our field, dropped into the grass and stared at the sky.

'I can't see it.'

'It's there,' she said, pointing upwards.

'I can see the cloud, but it's nothing like a face.'

'That's Cat Stevens. Trust me. I'm good at this sort of stuff.'

'There's no way that's a face.'

She looked across at me, a piece of grass hanging from her mouth, her nose freckles raised by the mid-day sun. 'You're hopeless. No imagination. I don't know why I put up with you.'

'My wit, charm and personality,' I offered.

She put her head on my chest and cuddled close. 'Yeah, maybe. Either that or your new car.'

I closed my eyes and let the sun soak into my face.

'What do you want to do with your life, Freddie?'

'Not thought about it.'

'You should. I want to get my degree, start my own business, travel; have a family – all sorts of things. Life's for living. My dad taught me that.'

'We should go,' I said. 'Mum will have cooked the dinner.'

She sighed. 'Just five more minutes.'

The second-hand 1600 GL Avenger cost me five hundred and forty pounds from Newtown Service Station. It had a rev counter with red digits next to the speedo. We stuck a Freddie and Jo-Jo sun-strip across the front windscreen. I bought a leather top for the gearstick and fitted a Sony radio cassette, with two speakers set up on the rear window shelf. Jo-Jo filled the back-seat with cuddly lions, dogs and cats. We used to park up down the lane next to Sam's caravan, three o'clock in the morning, fresh out of Max's, climb in the back seat and make love to Barbra Streisand's 'Guilty' album. One night Jo-Jo got drunk and slow-danced naked in front of the car headlights. I watched from the driver's seat, storing the memory for the rest of my life.

*Freddie – July 2015*

The coffee shop lunch-time crowd had assembled for their toasted sandwiches and homemade cakes. Some of the regulars were on their third cappuccino with chocolate sprinkles. The waitress came over and asked us if we wanted more drinks. We shook our heads and she moved on around the tables.

'Gets busy here,' said Jo-Jo.

'Everyday,' I said. 'We should have had another drink really.'

'They don't seem that bothered. Anyway, I haven't finished this one yet. You still haven't told me about your family.'

'Not much to tell.'

'Did you marry?'

'I came close. I have a daughter, Becky. She's grown up now. I don't see her much.'

'Jack said you live on your own.'

'Sounds like he gave you chapter and verse.'

'I might have asked,' she said.

I looked around the room. My eyes fell on two watercolours of a medieval church. Stella, the coffee shop owner, had bought them from a local artist. I picked up one of the paper napkins and turned it over in my hand.

'Jack's always been an old gossip,' I said. 'He wouldn't have needed much encouragement. Tell me about your daughter.'

'We're close, always have been.'

'What does she do?'

'She's a lawyer, got her own practice. Nicky, my grandson, he's ten and Sophia, my gorgeous granddaughter, is thirteen. She's fallen in love already. I told her, "Take your time. There's no rush."'

'Sounds wonderful. I can see why you want to be with them.'

'I don't go until the end of the month,' she said. 'Perhaps we could meet up, go for a meal, a bottle of wine.' She reached inside her bag and handed over a slip of paper. 'I've written down my address and phone number. Just in case you want to keep in touch. No pressure.'

'Of course,' I said. 'I will. I'll call.'

\*\*\*

The chair opposite me was empty. I looked again at the photo Jo-Jo had left behind. Thirty-five years. The lane and the field would still be there, but the Avenger was long gone. And Sam. And his greyhounds. And the pork pie hat. I finger traced Jo-Jo's photographic image, bringing her back to me. We were sitting in a photo booth; I was leaning in from the side. It had taken us ages to fix the stool at the right height, standing opposite each other, me turning it clockwise, Jo-Jo anti-clockwise. 'That's right. Leave it alone.' 'It isn't. It needs to come down more.' And then the wait outside. Spitting with rain. My anxiety. My anticipation. Would they come out okay? Our first pictures together, proof of a connection. The photos dropping into the metal grid; us waiting ten seconds whilst they dried. I'd tried not to smile too widely, embarrassed by my chipped front tooth. Jo-Jo was holding up two fingers in a peace sign, the camera had caught her glancing sideways at me. Her auburn hair. Her nose freckles. Why hadn't I kissed her when she'd left the coffee shop?

'You okay, Freddie?'

Tom. He was at my table again, his wife smiling anxiously across the room.

'I'm fine, Tom. Thanks for asking.'

'It's just that…well, we couldn't help noticing.'

The waitress came over. 'Another skimmed milk latte?' she said.

Everything had gone quiet, eyes at every table were looking at me – closing in on me. I shook my head, stood up and walked out of the shop.

*Jo-Jo – July 2015*

---

I turned right out of the coffee shop and walked along the high street to the pub car park where I'd left my panther black Mazda convertible. I pressed the key fob. The lights on the car flickered twice and I sat in the driver's seat, staring out at the playing fields. Freddie. I'd wanted him to hug me for longer, but he'd pulled away after a few seconds. He'd blushed when I'd kissed him on the cheek, his neck turning florid as though we'd been caught out in some major indecency. I smiled at the thought. Sweet. I'd said it all those years ago and I'd been right.

The passenger side door opened. Amy dropped in the seat next to me.

'Everything okay, Mum? Was he there?'

I nodded.

'What's he like? Was he pleased to see you?'

A noise from the park. A boy and a girl about seven years of age were being pushed on the swings by their mother. 'Higher, Mummy,' the girl shouted. 'I want to go higher.'

I pressed the power button and dabbed the accelerator with my right foot. The engine ignited. 'Put your seatbelt on,' I said.

'Mum. What did he say?'

'He said he'd ring.'

Amy shook her head, pulled the seatbelt across her body and clicked it in place.


*Jo-Jo – A Memory*

---

Amy is seven. I watch from the landing as she conducts a marriage ceremony for Sindy and Action Man in her bedroom. The Action Man belongs to her cousin, Thomas. It's the Eagle Eyes version whose creepy gaze follows you around the room. She places both dolls on the bed, standing them against her My Little Pony cushions. Sindy is dressed in a ballerina outfit with blue dancing slippers, white tights, a light blue leotard and a pink tutu skirt. Eagle Eyes is wearing full khaki combat dress with an American officers' cap placed on his head. Amy kneels on the floor in front of them.

'Do you, Eagle Eyes, take the beautiful and gorgeous Sindy to be your lawfully wedded wife?'

'I do,' says Amy in a deep, gruff voice.

She turns Action Man's eyes to face his soon to be bride. 'Let's get on with it. I've got a battle to fight.'

I put my hand to my mouth.

Amy tuts. 'Typical man, Mummy,' she says.

13

I nod, trying desperately not to laugh.

'We need to make you look presentable,' she says to Sindy, smoothing down the doll's blonde nylon hair. 'Do you, Sindy, take the rugged and handsome Eagle Eyes to be your lawfully wedded husband?'

'I do. I do. I do.'

Amy picks up both dolls.

'You may kiss the bride,' she declares, bringing Eagle Eyes and Sindy's faces together and looking up at me.

'They love each other, Mummy. They'll be together forever.'


## Jo-Jo – February 1980

Freddie and I were sitting side-by-side on a squishy white leather sofa in Max's games area. Freddie liked to get to the club early and play space invaders on the table-top Pac-Man before the crowds arrived. He was top scorer.

'Shouldn't we be going?' I said, stretching to look over the balcony at the dance floor. 'I want to eat before the Beatles Night starts.'

'In a minute,' he said, his eyes still fixed on the beeping screen.

I took a sip of my Pernod Crème-de-Menthe and flopped back in the chair, my black and white polka-dot Twiggy dress riding up my bare thighs.

'Do you like my dress?' I said.

He grunted.

'Dad gave me the money.'

Another grunt.

'And the Go-Go boots,' I said, putting my feet up on the Pac-Man.

He looked at the yellow boots and then at my thighs.

'You're blushing, Freddie.'

He took a quick look around the room, put his hand on my knee and traced a line up my right leg with his forefinger. He was grinning like a mischievous little boy who'd stolen a toffee. He stopped just under the hemline of my dress, leaned down and kissed me on the lips. 'You're beautiful,' he said.

I lightly pinched his sideburns. His breath smelt of aniseed. 'These are coming on. We'll soon have you looking like Ray Davies.' I tilted my head to one side and looked up at him, my eyes covered in thick black pencil liner and mascara. 'Can we eat now?'

'What do you fancy?' he said.

I pulled his head down and gave him a long, hard searching kiss.

*Jo-Jo – July 2015*

The Mazda purred effortlessly along the countryside lanes, acres and acres of fields streaming past the window, birdsong filling the car through the open roof. I thought of Dad and our endless day trips to dirty rain seaside towns: Borth, Rhyl, Aberystwyth. We did them all in his hearse-like brown Volvo; me and my younger brother, Josh, flicking at each other in the back seat, Dad giving us his rear view mirror glare, Mum passing round cheese and onion quarter cut sandwiches and orange pop in plastic cups to calm everyone down.

'Has he changed much?' said Amy.

'Not really,' I said. 'He's still Freddie.'

I turned on the radio. Jeremy Vine was interviewing a politician. 'So when exactly will that take place, Minister?' Amy switched the radio off.

'Tell me what you said to him, Mum.'

'I told him I was emigrating.'

'That must have shook him up.'

'Why? We haven't exactly kept in touch.'

'I bet he phones.'

'Maybe,' I said. 'We'll see.'

'You still care for him, don't you?'

'I'm not sure. We always just—'

'—You're not going to say clicked, are you?'

'I was going to say fitted.'

'Like comfy slippers,' she said. 'That's good. Now Dad's gone. Now you're—'

'—If you say old, you're walking to the hotel.'

'I was going to say mature.'

'That's worse. Makes me sound like a smelly cheese.'

'I'm just saying, I get it. No-one wants comfy slippers at eighteen. You want a pair of Jimmy Choo's. Florescent ones with five inch heels. But as you get older...'

'I might slap you in a minute.'

'He'll phone,' she said.


*Jo-Jo – May 1974*

---

We were all packed inside Dad's Volvo on our way to Aberystwyth. Drizzling rain had woken up the vegetation, leaving a freshly laundered sheen on the world. Mum had pointed out the sheep and cows in the fields like they were exotic herds roaming the land, Josh and I grunting acknowledgements from the back seat. I'd read my Jackie magazine over and over and we'd eaten two packets of Marks and Spencer's mint humbugs. Dad had spent most of the journey singing his way through the Beatles greatest hits and we'd all joined in with the choruses.

'There's the sea,' said Dad.

I craned my neck to look.

'I can see it,' said Josh.

'No you can't,' I said.

'You'll both be able to see in a minute,' said Mum.

We turned a corner and there it was. I'd built it up in my head as an azure water carpet stretching out to the horizon, but it was more battleship grey with dirty white flecks on the tips of the waves. I felt sad to see the end of the land, the end of our journey.

Dad parked the Volvo and pushed some coins into one of the parking meters. 'That'll give us a couple of hours,' he said. Mum stood me and Josh in front of her, pulled the Parka hoods over our heads and zipped the coats tight under our chins. 'Don't take them off,' she warned us. 'You'll catch your death. And put your gloves on.'

Mum and Dad walked in front of us along the seafront, Dad holding their umbrella, me holding ours. I hummed 'A Hard Day's Night' and Dad joined in. Mum tutted and I looked at Josh. He shrugged and ran into one of the open-fronted arcades, bells and flashing lights beating out from every direction, a faint odour of sweat and dirty coins. An unshaven man with uncombed hair, grass stained track-suit bottoms and a hooded sweat-top, slapped the side of a fruit machine in frustration. 'Oi, mate,' boomed a voice. I looked around. The change counter woman, standing inside a Perspex box, leaned again into her mike. 'Do that again,' she said, 'and you're out.' The man smiled, kicked the front of the machine and ran out of the arcade. 'Dick,' said the woman.

Josh sat down behind the steering wheel of the Grand Prix machine and looked hopefully at Mum. She walked over and pushed a two pence coin into the slot. The screen lit up.

Dad and I closed the umbrellas. We walked over to the machine and watched in silence as Josh turned the wheel, laughing and steering his way around a Formula One track, the sounds of tyre screeches and exhaust acceleration coming from the simulated Lotus.

Mum rubbed the back of Josh's head. 'Well done, darling,' she said.

I looked at Dad and raised my eyebrows. He smiled and squeezed my hand.

## Jo-Jo – January 1972

I blew out the ten pink candles on my princess birthday cake and Dad handed me a long rectangular box, which he'd wrapped the night before in Snoopy wrapping paper. I read the card.

'*To our darling daughter, Jo-Jo.*
*Happy Birthday*
*All our love*
*Mum and Dad*
*XXXX*'

'I don't know why you've bought her that,' said Mum. 'She won't use it.'

'I will,' I said, tearing at the wrapping paper. 'What is it?'

'It's a telescope,' said Josh.

Dad glared at him. 'And it's meant to be a surprise.'

I looked at the uncovered box. It had a picture of the night sky with shooting stars, moons, rushing meteors and 'Stargazer' written across its full length in gold lettering.

'A telescope?' I said.

'We can set it up in your room,' said Dad. 'It's got its own tripod.'

I opened the box and pulled out the white telescope.

'She hates it,' said Mum.

'I love it,' I said.

Dad grinned and handed me a second present. It was a hardback book entitled, 'Exploring the Universe'. 'It tells us what to look for,' he said.

I kissed him on the cheek. 'Thank you, Dad.'


*Jo-Jo – August 1972*

---

We were at my cousin Tanya's wedding. Waltz music started up and Dad put his arm around my waist and twirled me across the dance-floor.

'One, two three. One, two three.'

I could feel Mum watching, and Josh.

'One, two, three. One, two three.'

Dad spun me faster and faster. My first pair of high-heeled shoes were slipping off my feet and I had to concentrate really hard to keep up with him. 'Don't let him down,' I told myself. I held my head back and closed my eyes. I opened my eyes. The mirror balls, the laughter from everyone around us, the smell of Dad's tangy Aramis aftershave. The music changed. We stopped dancing. The room carried on spinning.

'That was great, Dad.'

'You're a natural,' he said. 'We'll get you some classes sorted.'

'Really. When? When can we start?'

Mum walked over and hugged me.

'Dad's going to teach me to dance. Aren't you, Dad?'


*Jo-Jo – February 1980*

---

We had to make our way down two spiral staircases to reach Max's basement restaurant. The area around the dance floor had filled up. A gang of lads at the bar stared at us as we came down the first flight. I smiled at them, praying all the time to stay upright in the Go-Go boots. Freddie kept his eyes fixed on the steel steps. He was wearing the outfit I'd chosen for him: a slim cut black suit; highly polished Chelsea boots; a sky blue Oxford shirt with a button down collar, and a tightly knotted pencil tie. I'd gone with him the previous afternoon to get his hair cut, pointing out John Lennon's mop top style from a copy of 'Face' magazine. 'That one,' I'd said. 'That's the one he wants.'

The waiter hurried over as we walked through the saloon style swing doors. He showed us to our table and we gave him our order. Freddie rearranged his cutlery.

'Why do you do that?' I said.

'My mum's left handed.'

'But you're right handed.'

'Apart from using a knife and fork.'

The Muscadet arrived.

'Would madam like to taste?' said the waiter.

I took a sip and nodded.

'I always expect you to send that back,' said Freddie.

'One of these days, I will.'

'I'd die,' he said. 'I'd rather pay for it.'

The food arrived.

'Don't,' I said.

'What?'

'You're about to say what you always say. It drives me mad.'

'I was just wondering how you can eat steak like that.'

'Like what?'

'Your plate's full of blood. It's soaking into your chips.'

I forked a piece of the T-Bone into my mouth and began to slowly chew. 'It's yummy,' I said. 'You don't know what you're missing.'

'Blood, mainly, by the looks of it.'

'No point in having a steak if you're going to cook all the good out of it. That's what my dad tells me. How's your chicken?'

'My 'chicken chasseur' is fine. At least it's cooked.'

'Do you want to try my steak?'

'No thanks.'

I forked another piece of meat and waved it under his nose. 'Go on. Get some proper food inside you.'

'I think you're a vampire,' he said.

I bared my teeth and growled at him. 'You'd like that wouldn't you.'

'What?'

'Me dressed as a vampire and biting you.'

He poured some wine into my glass. 'Maybe,' he said.

I laughed. 'Try this piece of steak and I might think about it.'

*Jo-Jo – Freddie's Book*

---

Freddie used to write short stories. I pestered him for weeks until he finally relented and read one to me in my bedroom. 'Are you sure you want to hear this, Jo-Jo?'

'Yes. I want to hear it.'

'It's rubbish,' he said.

'Read it, Freddie. I want to know what happens.'

The main character, Chardonnay, committed suicide, leaving no note and her heartbroken soul mate, Jacob, desperate to know the reason why. Luther, an Arbiter from the afterlife, visited Jacob, saying he would explain everything. The whole thing was being played on a big screen to a packed stadium full of gods, who were laughing, eating pies and sipping home-made punch – a big show with a circus, carnivals, fairs and bric-a-brac stalls. In the end, Jacob took his own life, thinking it would lead to Chardonnay, but he turned to dust and the gods moved on with their next episode.

I turned the Mazda into the conifer-framed entrance of the Hotel Rushmore, dropped the car into second gear and crept along the narrow privet hedged lane. Flashes of sunlight streaked through the trees, reflecting off the windscreen. The car was moving from dark to light, dark to light. I wanted to sneeze, but I pushed the thought away and concentrated on avoiding any overhanging branches. I didn't want to scratch the car. It was the only thing I'd bought for myself out of Jason's insurance money.

'You'd think they'd have better access,' I said, my eyes fixed on the tarmac.

'Strange name for a hotel,' said Amy.

The car hit a pothole and bounced to the right. I jerked the steering wheel to correct it.

'What?' I said.

'The hotel. The receptionist told me the owner wanted a reminder of her holiday in New York.'

'But Mount Rushmore's in Dakota.'

'I think she just wanted something American.'

We pulled out of the lane and into the driveway sweep in front of the Georgian house. I parked up in one of the guest spaces and unclicked my seatbelt.

'I'm not sure I'll be that bothered if he doesn't phone,' I said.

'Stop worrying, Mum. I think you're the best thing that's ever happened to him.'

I looked at her. 'What a strange thing to say.'

'Does he have a family?' she said.

'A daughter. He doesn't see her.'

'And this Jack fellow's his only mate?'

'You make him sound really sad.'

'All I'm saying is, he'll phone. I bet there's a message at reception.'

'And then what?'

'I don't know, Mum. Whatever you want.'

*Jo-Jo – April 1980*

---

The fairground was humming with conversation, the smell of frying doughnuts and hot dogs with onions laced the air, and the Boomtown Rats' 'I Don't Like Mondays' was blasting out through the music system. I grabbed Freddie's arm and pulled him through the crowd to the waltzers.

We dropped into one of the cars and I snuggled into his chest. One of the ride attendants jumped on the back and grinned down at us. He had a gold sovereign ring on his right hand and a red-faced pirate tattoo on his forearm. 'You two okay?' he said. We looked up at him and nodded. Freddie pulled a crumbled one-pound note from his trouser pocket and handed it over. The attendant gave him a fifty pence piece out of his money bag. 'Nice hat,' he said, before jumping to the walzter next door.

'See,' I said.

'He was taking the piss,' said Freddie. 'I'm taking it off.'

'You can't. It was a present. You look good. Sexy.'

'Really?'

'Really.'

He grinned. The ride started. Freddie pressed the Mod hat down on his head.

'Make sure it doesn't blow off,' I said.

*Jo-Jo – July 2015*

---

We climbed the hotel steps and entered the reception area, me wearily following Amy. She strode across the lobby's thick pile carpet, her heels leaving a trail of indentations in the beige wool. I saw the nervy young male receptionist spot her heading his way. He straightened up in his chair and beamed out his best greeting smile like a defence shield. He looked like he was about to be held up at gun point.

'Good morning, madam,' he stuttered. 'Can I help you?'

'You have a message for my mother,' she said. 'Mrs Coulman. Room 242.'

'Of course,' he said. 'I'll check.'

Amy drummed her fingers on the desk as he tapped away at the keyboard in front of him. I gave her a glare and she stopped.

'I'm sorry,' said the receptionist. 'There's no message.'

'Can you check again?'

He looked back at his computer screen. 'No,' he said. 'There's nothing against that name. Were you told there was?'

'We just thought there might be,' I said. 'Thank you for looking.'

Amy turned to me and shrugged. 'He'll call later,' she said. 'What do you want to do this afternoon, Mum?'

'I'm going up to have a lie down. Do you mind? I feel exhausted.'

She touched my arm, gave me a sympathetic look. 'Of course not. You go and have a rest. We'll meet up in a couple of hours.'

'What about you?'

'I might give Dan a call. See how the kids are.'

'You can't phone now. It's after midnight over there.'

She pulled an iPhone out of her Gucci handbag and walked towards the conservatory. 'Later, Mum,' she said, putting her hand in the air.

'I wish I had that confidence,' said the receptionist.

I looked at him. He blushed and looked back at his screen.

'She gets it off her father,' I said.

'Would you like to book a call for four o'clock, madam?'

I smiled. 'Yes,' I said. 'Thank you. A call's a good idea.'

## Jo-Jo – April 1980

We stood still for a few seconds to regain our balance after the waltzer ride. The attendant had perched himself on the back of our car and spun us around and around and around. 'I think he was trying to knock your hat off,' I said.

'Still here though,' said Freddie, lifting up his hat in salute.

I grabbed his hand and nodded towards the Shoot a Duck stall. 'Come on. You can win me one of those bears.'

He groaned. 'Jo-Jo, they're fixed.'

'I thought you were good at that stuff. Mr Pac-Man-Top-Scorer.'

'That's different.'

'Well, if you're not up to it...'

'I didn't say that.'

We ran over to the stall. Freddie handed over his money.

'What you after?' said the stall holder, picking up his greasy beef burger and taking a bite.

"He's going to win me the bear," I said, pointing at the three foot high white teddy bear perched on the top shelf. The bear had a gold star pinned to his chest with 'Star Prize' written in red felt tip pen.

The Shoot a Duck man stopped chewing and looked at Freddie, who was already taking aim through the sights of the rifle.

'You need all six on target to win a bear, mate.'

'He knows,' I said.

Ten minutes later, we walked away from the stall, me

25

clutching a five inches high brown teddy bear, Freddie with a scowl across his face.

'I told you it was fixed,' he said.

'You got all six ducks.'

'Yeah, and then he pulls that, "Sign says win a bear. It don't say which bear," routine.'

'You're still my hero,' I said, kissing the bear. 'And now, Mr Rifleman, you owe me a candyfloss. A pink one.'

## Jo-Jo – July 2015

My mum gave me the oriental carpet bag on my sixteenth birthday. She came into the kitchen, still in her dressing gown, and dropped it in the middle of the dining table. 'Look after it,' she said. 'It was your granny's.' It was edged with gold stitching and had a satin image of two geisha girls standing in a garden of Eucalyptus trees, bowing serenely at the world. When I went to Blackpool with Freddie it held my Sony Walkman and transistor radio; in the Hotel Rushmore it held my iPod and Kindle.

I pulled the bag down from the top shelf of the wardrobe, unzipped one of the side pockets and retrieved a red leather photograph album. Three pages in, I found Jason's list. He'd written it with a 15 karat gold fountain pen given to him by the university when he retired. Josh used to tease him, saying he must be the last person in England to use real ink.

Things I love about Jo-Jo

1. Our holidays in the Indian Ocean
2. Watching you sleep
3. Watching you catwalk through La Rambla Boulevard in your red evening dress

4. Our dances – me holding you closer and closer
5. Talcum powdered sheets
6. Meals on the beach
7. All the men staring in envy at me
8. You decorating the Christmas tree, everything co-ordinated

I'd read the list over and over since his death, but I still couldn't work out why he'd written it. Wishful thinking, romanticism of what he really wanted but could never achieve. 'That's so sweet,' Amy had said when we'd found it his desk drawer. It was all lies. He thought the beach meals were chilly, the red dress was showy and he was far too self-conscious to enjoy our dances. 'I bet they think you're my nurse,' he'd say when we were out together. He used to sit for hours with his head buried in a book, paralysed by his own inadequacies, real life passing him by at express train speed. 'If only,' was his mantra. 'If only I were twenty years younger.'

'You said that twenty years ago,' I'd answer. He gave me security, stability and, eventually, Amy. I got used to the rest.

*Jo-Jo – Jason's Routines*

1. Saturday night Monopoly with our neighbours, Alex and Julie – Jason the Top Hat; me the Iron; him the Banker and Sommelier, me the nibbles and things on sticks provider.
2. Sunday lunch at the Horse and Jockey, him beef, me pork (the look on his face when I announced my conversion to vegetarianism), two bottles of Merlot limit (any more would be reckless), his raised eyebrows when I moved on to Gin and Tonics, him studiously reading the broadsheets, critiquing the state of the nation, me pressing his buttons by bringing him up-to-date with the gossip columns – 'Can't you read that rubbish quietly?'

3. Tea on the table at five-thirty, even after he'd retired – 'It gives us a chance to get ready for the news.'
4. Him retiring to his office to audit our joint bank account, ticking off every item, filing them away in date order, separate folders for each financial year, after year, after year, waving statements in my face, questioning me about every purchase – 'What did you draw another twenty pounds out for?' Can't you take sandwiches to work?' 'They weren't for me, Jason. I treated my lover.'

*Jo-Jo – July 1976*

Miss Giles, our English teacher, had let us leave school early and I was back at home, watching Dad through the kitchen window. I was counting down from ten, giving Dad's declared sixth sense a chance to kick itself into action. I reached six before he looked up from his rose pruning and grinned. I ran outside and within seconds I was lifted skywards in his muscular arms, sucking in the leathery tang of his gardening day sweat.

'How did you know I was here?'

'I always know,' he said, putting me back on planet earth and ruffling my hair. 'How was school? It was English today wasn't it?'

'I'll do well to get the O level, Dad.'

'Oh, you'll get it. You're going to write a book. I can feel it in my bones.'

I looked back towards the house. 'Where's Mum?'

'In bed,' he muttered, the smile disappearing from his face. 'She's had a bad day. Go and see her.'

'I've got homework to do.'

'Jo-Jo, you know she watches the clock until you get home. Just go and say hello.'

'Do I have to? I never know what to say.'

He turned me around and pushed me gently up the garden. 'Go now,' he said. 'I'll get the tea on.'

I trudged up the path and into the kitchen, shedding motivation with every step as I walked into the hallway and started up the stairs. I stopped and looked up at the landing, pictures of long dead relatives hanging along the flocked wallpaper route. 'For God's sake, Jo-Jo,' I said to myself. 'You're only going to say hello to Mum.'

'Hello, Mum.'

'Is that you, Jo-Jo?'

I was leaning against the open door to Mum's room, her infantile voice creeping out from under a duck feather duvet. Two years she'd been ill. What was wrong with her? Schizophrenia, Dad called it.

'Jesus, Mum. It's like a sauna in here.'

'I feel the cold,' she said. 'You know I feel the cold.'

I walked into the bedroom and yanked the curtains open, dust shimmering into the room, sunlight exploding onto the bed. Mum screamed.

'Oh my God, close the curtains. Please close the curtains.'

I pulled the curtains back together.

'What wrong, Mum?' I said, sitting down on the bed. 'It's a lovely day. I can't see how lying in the dark is going to help.'

'I'm sorry, sweetheart,' she said, sweat beads glistening on her forehead. 'It's been a bad day.'

'Let me turn the heating down. You're ringing wet.'

'No, darling. Just sit and talk to me.'

I lifted a flannel from the bowl of water Dad kept by the side of the bed, squeezed it out, and gently wiped Mum's brow. I looked across at the curtains, double checking they were closed. 'I must try harder,' I told myself. 'I must try to understand.'

'She'll be okay. I'm going to the doctors tomorrow.'

Dad was filling the space in the doorway. I guessed that Mum's scream had brought him sprinting upstairs. 'But you're at work tomorrow,' I said.

'They'll understand. I'll make it up at the weekend.'

'You're working at the weekend,' said Mum. 'What about the shopping, Joseph? Who's going to do the shopping? I can't do it. You know I can't do it. Please don't ask me to do it.'

He walked over to the bed and took Mum's hand. 'Calm down, love. I'm going to the shop after work.'

'What about the tea? Who's going to get Jo-Jo's tea?'

'I'll get my own tea,' I said. 'I'm not the one who's useless, and it sounds like Dad's got enough to do.'

'Get out,' screamed Mum. 'Just go, leave me alone. Both of you leave me alone. You don't understand. I'm not well. I need rest. Leave me alone.'

'Fine,' I said. 'I've got homework to do anyway.'

*Jo-Jo – October 1977*

I'd walked into town to get some fresh air, taking a break from revising for my O level mock exams. I came out of the newsagents, where I'd stopped off to buy a can of Pepsi, and saw Dad striding through the green entrance gates of the park. He stopped at one of the wooden benches, sat down and placed his Dunlop golfing umbrella at his side. He stood up again almost immediately and put up his hand in greeting. A woman, walking towards him, waved back. Dad walked towards her, leaving his umbrella on the bench. They came together, hugged, and then kissed a thirty second kiss on the lips. Dad touched the woman's cheek, looked into her eyes and said something. The woman nodded. They held hands and walked back to the bench. The woman said something to Dad and he laughed. They reached the bench, sat down, still holding hands, still talking, still smiling; still laughing.

I walked across the road and into the park. Dad saw me as I came through the gates and he jumped up off the bench. The woman looked at him with concerned eyes and then looked at me.

'Hello, Dad.'

'Jo-Jo. What are you doing here?'

'I thought you were at your evening class,' I said.

'It was cancelled.'

I held out my hand towards the woman. 'I'm his daughter. I don't think we've met.'

She stood up and kissed Dad on the cheek. 'I think it's best if I go, Joseph. Give me a call later.' He nodded and she walked away, out of the park. Dad watched her go and then picked up his umbrella.

'I don't want to talk about this, Jo-Jo,' he said, staring at the bench.

'Who is she?'

'A friend.'

'She looked like more than a friend. Is it serious?'

'Jo-Jo, you're fifteen, old enough to understand. I needed some company and she was there.'

'Does Mum know?'

'No,' he said. 'But I don't think she'd care if she did.'

'I can't believe this, Dad. This isn't you.'

He pulled me close and kissed the top of my head. 'I love you, Jo-Jo,' he said.

I pushed him away. 'What about Mum?'

'I'll always love your mother —'

'Are you going to leave us?' I said, tears welling in my eyes.

'Leave you? Of course I'm not going to leave you.'

Back in my room at the Hotel Rushmore, I lay on the bed and stared at the L.S. Lowry print on the bedroom wall. A picture of a man standing on the beach, looking out at a cloudless sky and calm sea. He had his hands shoved into his suit trouser pockets and two black and white terrier dogs were facing up to each other behind him.

I remembered Dad watching the tide come in, the waves encroaching slowly up the beach, consuming the sandy moats and turrets that he'd spent all afternoon building with me and Josh. Mum used to lie on her sun lounger and shout instructions – 'That end needs to be higher.' 'You need more of a mound there.' We'd ask her to join in. 'I'm here to look glamorous,' she'd say. 'Like Brigitte bloody Bardot,' Dad would answer, making Mum laugh.

Dad taught me and Josh the symptoms of schizophrenia and the side-effects of Mum's tablets. Josh used to run around our front room with a sheet over him making spooky ghost noises. 'Oooh… Mum's voices have got me. The voices…oooh…I can't stand the voices.' If Dad caught him he'd cuff him lightly across the back of his head. 'Show some bloody respect,' he'd say, but he'd wink at me as he was doing it. Dad made Mum get up, get dressed and come downstairs. She always protested. 'I can't, Joseph. You know I can't.'

'Yes you can, love. Today's a good day and you can.'

The phone rang at the side of the bed, making me jump. I reached over and picked up the receiver.

'Hello.'

'Mrs Coulman?'

I recognised the shy receptionist's hesitant voice. 'Yes,' I said.

'I'm sorry to disturb you, madam, but there is a message for you. It had been put in the wrong box. You see all the rooms have their own mailbox —'

'What's the message?' I said.

*Freddie's Morning Regime*

---

1. I wake-up early, turn on my side, pull the mustard coloured candlewick bedspread under my chin and watch the red digits on the bedside clock tick over to alarm time, forcing myself to stay in bed until Springsteen's 'Thunder Road' starts the day

2. I listen out for Georgie, my neighbour's Basset Hound. No howling means she isn't in the house. I imagine her out on her morning walk, sniffing down a scent in the local park, her ears trailing a path through the dew covered grass. The image makes me smile. She'll be back soon, reenergised by the fresh air, ready to face another day on her own while Tracey, her owner, is out at work in the local care home. Georgie's howling doesn't bother me. It interrupts the various moods of loneliness that possess every room in my mum's three bedroom semi like uninvited guests.

3. Bruce's harmonica breaks the silence, triggering me to get up, open the curtains; walk downstairs to let the cats out – the only other heartbeats in the house since Mum's death. All four of them appear from their various sleeping places and head for the back door.

4. I shower, dress and go through my leaving the house ritual, starting in the kitchen, moving from room to room, checking the plugs are out, running my hand under all the taps, making sure there's an even spread of curtain on each side of the windows, locking and unlocking

the back door, counting out loud, one, two, three, four, moving the handle up and down after each turn of the key, repeating the routine with the front door – out in the street, exposed.

*Freddie – July 2015*

---

When Jack and I were kids, I used to sing-song the names of his fifteen siblings in age order. My mum used to let him have his tea at our house – 'It'll save him getting in the queue over there.' She'd give him my old socks, which he was forever losing – 'Our Malcolm pinched them, Mrs B.'

'Never mind, lad. Go and get yourself another pair out of Freddie's drawer.' At fourteen, we started wagging days off school, hiding away in my house to plot our big ideas. We were going to form a band, sail around the world, write a best-seller. We also made lists of girls we fancied. Jack used to lie on my mum's leather settee and I'd sit in the armchair with my feet up on a footstool, both of us wearing Ian Dury granddad caps and flared Levis, chewing on BIC biros and staring at our hardback notebooks.

'Sharon Terry,' I said. 'She should be on your list.'

'Why?'

'She likes you.'

'This is stupid, Freddie. I've got twenty-five names on here.'

'Once we've got a list we can come up with a strategy. See how that goes.'

'It's not a battle plan.'

'Preparation's everything, my friend.'

'You know Wilkes has got a girl now?' said Jack.

'Smelly Wilkes?'

'Yeah.'

'Who'd go out with him?'

'Yvonne Mason.'

'Proves my point. No plan and you end up with buck teeth and glasses.'

'Yeah, well. At least he's not making bloody lists.'

*Freddie – October 1986*

H.I.V. tombstone adverts, the world getting over macho man Rock Hudson dying of AIDS, Boy George having a lifestyle melt down with his new beau, Marilyn, and the Chief Constable of Greater Manchester Police describing gay men as 'swirling in a cesspit of their own making'. This was the year Jack came out. It was like he looked at the headlines and thought, 'Fuck it.'

He told his mum and dad over a pot of tea and a Mr Kipling victoria sandwich. His mum kissed him on the forehead, told him to be careful. His dad didn't say a word. 'I'll never forget the look of disappointment on his face,' Jack told me.

Jack took his mouthy sister, Jackie, to the Mason's Arms and bought her a G & T – 'I knew she'd tell all the others before I got back to the house,' he said. The rest of his siblings took the piss: 'Fancy our kid being a big poof'; 'Hey, Jackie, hide your dresses. He'll be after them.' In the pub someone shouted 'Fairy' and Jack's brother, Malcolm, walked over and punched the bloke in the face. 'You call it him,' said the barman. 'That's different,' said Malcolm, the whole pub looking at him. 'We're family. You lot leave him alone.'

Jack told me over a pint of Guinness and a game of darts.

'Gay?'

'Yeah. You know what that means, Freddie?'

'Sort of.'

'It doesn't mean I fancy you.'

I walked to Jack's house from the coffee shop. We only lived three streets apart, but he'd insisted on a schedule for keeping in touch – a curry at the Saleem Bagh on the last Friday of the month and a weekly, Wednesday night catch up on the phone. 'I love you to bits, Freddie, but I need some space.'

'You make it sound like we're married.'

'You mean we're not?' I knew his rules were flexible, though, and I could always break them in an emergency.

I pressed the front doorbell. Jack's ginger tomcat, Boris, who was dozing on the front lawn, opened his one eye and looked at me with suspicion, daring me to disturb his morning. A silver Ford Fiesta pulled up at the house opposite. A nurse in uniform got out of the car and ran up the path. She was a midwife visiting Jack's neighbour, Sandra, who was expecting her third child.

Jack opened his door. 'Freddie,' he said. 'Come in.'

I followed him down the hallway. 'I've just seen Jo-Jo,' I said. 'Why didn't you tell me you'd met up with her?'

'I forgot. It was only last week. I've just made coffee. Do you want some?'

We walked into his lounge and sat down opposite each other in his blue leather bucket seats from Next. Paul Weller's 'Wild Wood' was humming away in the corner from a Bose sound dock. The room had no ornaments, pictures or mirrors. Stainless steel spotlights were fixed at uniform gaps across the white ceiling.

'What were you doing at a charity event?' I said.

'I do have a life beyond you, Freddie.'

I handed him the picture. 'She gave me that.'

He wolf whistled. 'Nice hair. That cut was always underrated.'

'You had it as well,' I said. 'Before you turned all Erasure on us.'

He grinned, turned the picture over and read aloud the

inscription on the back: 'Freddie and Me. Blackpool. 1980. DTR.' He looked at me. 'DTR?'

'She used to rate her pictures. DTR: Days to Remember or DTF: Days to Forget.'

'Well, at least you got top billing, darling.'

He only ever called me darling when he was being sarcastic and I didn't want him taking the piss out of the picture. I held out my hand and he passed it back to me.

'She brought me this photo,' I said. 'And then told me she was emigrating.'

'I don't see the problem.'

'It's a bit odd, don't you think, turning up after thirty-five years. She wants me to phone her and meet up for a meal.'

He pushed the plunger down on his 'Café Bohème' cafetière, which was positioned in the centre of a glass topped coffee table.

'Give her a call,' he said. 'What have you got to lose?'


*Freddie – July 1997*

---

It was the third night of our stay in Sitges and we were on the terrace of the Hotel Romántico, the Catalonia air laced with a fruity aroma of lemon and lime trees, a droning background soundtrack of chirping male cicadas looking for a mate. Jack and the four guys we'd met two hours earlier in the bar were sitting around a large bamboo table. I was lying on a sun lounger, listening in on their conversation. We were slowly working our way through four carafes of the bar manager's Sangria special.

'How did you two meet?' said Jack, directing his question at Bob, the short, plump one with a receding hairline who'd told us he was a teacher.

'You tell them,' Bob said to his partner, Terry. 'You're the star man.'

'Don't build him up too much,' said Patrick. 'He doesn't look like top billing material to me.'

Patrick was the hotel's karaoke star. He dressed up every night in a ball gown and tiara to give his rendition of Freddie Mercury's 'God Save the Queen.' His cheeks were still covered in red rouge, but he was now wearing a white sweat vest bearing a cartoon image of fornicating hedgehogs and the legend, 'Be Careful of the Pricks.' He responded to Bob's hard glare by holding up his hands, palms outwards. 'Sorry,' he said. 'I'll not say another word.'

'Yeah, right,' said Terry.

Patrick went to reply, but his partner Mickey put a hand on his arm. 'Just let him tell the bloody story,' he said.

Terry took a sip of his Sangria. 'Not much to tell really. I was fifty-five, had a wife, kids, and grandkids, and then he turned up.' He nodded at Bob. 'I'd been watching him for months before I asked him out for a coffee. Next thing I know, I'm announcing us to the world.'

'That must have been tough,' said Jack.

'It was a relief to be honest. I'd got sick of living the lie.'

'Do you still see your kids?' I said.

All five of them turned and faced me. I think they'd forgotten I was there.

Terry shook his head. 'Jemma, my daughter, writes, but my two sons have blanked me. They won't let me see the grandkids.'

'You will,' said Bob. 'They'll come round.'

'No chance,' said Patrick, stirring the fruit in his Sangria with an umbrella cocktail stick. 'They'll be too busy crucifying you.'

Terry stood up and walked into the bar. Bob followed him.

'You're an insensitive prat sometimes,' said Mickey.

'What? It's true.'

'Yeah, but you don't always have to say it.'

\*\*\*

6.00 P.M. the following evening. I was sitting in the piano bar, sipping an ice-cold San Miguel. Jack was out on a trip to Barcelona and I'd spent the day sunbathing by the pool, reading J.K. Rowling's 'Harry Potter and the Philosopher's Stone.' It was early and the bar was empty. Terry walked in, saw me and put up his hand. He walked over and sat down on the stool next to me.

'I'll have one of those,' he said to the barman, pointing at my chill frosted glass.

'How's it going?' I said.

He swallowed a gulp of beer. 'God, that's good' he said, lifting up his glass in my direction. We clinked our glasses together. 'Grimsby,' he said. We laughed.

'Where's your mate?' said Terry.

'He's off seeing the sights. Where's Bob?'

'Glamming himself up. He'll be down in a minute.'

We took a sip of our beers.

He wiped his mouth with the back of his hand. 'Sorry about last night,' he said.

'Nothing to be sorry for. Patrick's a prat.'

He nodded. 'Maybe, but he's right. They are going to crucify me.'

I took another sip of beer and stared at the yellow and red horizontal stripes painted on the wall behind the bar. Two black and white pictures of a 1930's bullfight hung on each side of the stripes. They showed a matador with one hand behind his back, facing up to a bull in different olè poses. The bull had his head bowed and looked as though he was scraping at the dusty ground and snorting out his frustration.

'Do you mind if I ask you a question?' I said.

'Ask away.'

'Do you regret leaving them?'

'If you mean my family, they left me.'

'I mean your wife. You left her for Bob.'

'The only regret I have is hurting the kids and not being honest with myself years ago. It's nothing to do with Bob.'

'But you love him, right?'

He laughed. 'Yeah,' he said. 'Whatever that means.' He tore the beer mat in half. 'You ever been in love?'

'Once,' I said.

'Are you still together?'

I shook my head. 'We split up when we were kids, wanted different things. She went off to university.'

'And?' he said.

'And nothing. We lost contact. It fizzled out.'

***

Jack and I walked back to the hotel along the harbour front, returning from our nightly residence in the Blue Oyster Cult nightclub in the centre of Sitges, where we watched Patrick deliver his main drag act performance before his finale back at the hotel. I'd been drinking pints of San Miguel since meeting Terry in the bar, but Jack was having one of his orange juice nights – 'It helps to clear out the system, darling.'

I suddenly had an urge to jump up on the seafront wall.

'What are doing, Freddie? Get down.'

I looked up at the night sky and sucked in the sea air.

'If we died now, Jack, I'd be happy.'

'That's because you're drunk.'

I held my arms out to my sides, tightrope walker style, and stepped carefully along the wall. 'See. I can walk the line. That means I'm perfectly sober.'

'Yeah, right. And I'm the Queen's granny.'

'You need to lighten up, Jack. You're getting old. You can't stand the pace.'

'You'll be sick in a minute, Freddie. Just after you fall off that wall.'

I gave him a sideways glance, stumbled, adjusted my balance and then glared at him.

'What?' he said. 'It's true. You're always sick.'

'That's because I'm a sensitive soul. If you paid me more attention you'd know.'

He laughed and held out his hand. 'All right. You've made your point. Now get down off that bloody wall before you do some damage.'

I grabbed his hand and jumped down in front of him. 'Why aren't you nicer to me, Jack?' I looked straight into his eyes. 'How come you never make a pass at me?'

His eyes dropped. 'Not this again, Freddie.'

I touched his unshaven cheek, lifted his chin and gently traced my forefinger around his lips. 'Kiss me,' I said. 'Just once. I want to know what it feels like.'

He pulled his hand out of my grasp and walked away.

'What's wrong with me?' I said, sitting down on the wall.

He turned back to face me. 'You're not gay, Freddie. You're drunk and lonely.'

'I love you, Jack,' I shouted.

He smiled, walked back to me and ruffled my hair. 'No you don't,' he said. 'But it's sweet of you to think you do.' He pulled me to my feet, put his arm around my waist and we started to walk.

'I think I'm going to be sick,' I said.

'Course you are,' he said, guiding me back towards the wall.

*Freddie – July 2015*

---

I closed my eyes and let Weller's throaty vocals fill my head. 'Wild Wood' had morphed into 'Shout to the Top' by the Style Council.

41

'What about if it's a sympathy thing?' I said, opening my eyes.

Jack sat back in the bucket seat. 'What?' he said.

'The redundancy, living on my own. She probably thinks I'm some sort of sad loser in need of her charity.'

'Aren't you?'

'Piss off,' I said.

He leaned forward in his chair. 'Did you tell her about the redundancy?'

'No. But I bet you did.'

'The point is, she was already looking for you. She didn't know anything about your life, but she was looking for you. Doesn't that say something?'

'Maybe.'

'You can be such a wanker sometimes. She's asked you out for a goodbye meal. She doesn't want to marry you or have your babies.' He picked up his iPhone and threw it into my lap. 'Call her. Use my phone.'

I turned the phone over in my hand.

'I swear to God, Freddie, I'll call her if you don't. And that'll make you look a right prick.'

He stood up and walked into the kitchen. I followed him. He put the coffee cups into the Belfast sink and threw a paisley tea-towel in my direction. 'You're drying,' he said. I ignored him, sat down on one of the breakfast bar stools and started flicking through the culture section of the Guardian newspaper. The front door opened. Bob walked down the hallway. He was wearing a light brown corduroy suit, desert boots and a red Panama hat, which he'd taken to after watching the first Indiana Jones film. I knew Bob visited, but I didn't know Jack had given him a key.

'Morning,' said Bob, dropping his hat on the breakfast bar and pulling out a packet of 'More' menthol cigarettes from his jacket pocket. He shook the packet in Jack's direction.

Jack sighed, opened the cupboard door under the sink and fetched out an amber coloured bubble glass ashtray in the shape of a duck, which he handed to Bob. 'I can't believe I let you smoke those things in here,' he said.

Bob took the ashtray, lit his cigarette and nodded at the kettle. 'Any chance of a coffee?' he said. 'Don't forget I'm back on sugar.'

\*\*\*

Jack made Bob put out his cigarette in the kitchen and we walked back into the lounge. Bob and I were carrying a mug of coffee; Jack was carrying a cup of liquorice tea. I smiled as we sat down on the bucket chairs. It really did feel like Jack was offering therapy appointments. Jackie used to tell him off. 'You shouldn't let people dump all their problems on you,' she'd say, and then she'd tell him about her latest love crisis. 'He's left me. Gone back to his wife.' 'That's what married men do, Sis.'

'How's Terry?' I said.

'He doesn't recognise me,' said Bob.

Jack was one of the first people Bob called when Terry had his stroke. 'You're a social worker. What do we do?' They'd found him a care home twenty minutes away.

'Any sign of the family?' said Jack.

'The daughter phones but nothing else.'

I thought of Patrick's prophecy all those years ago.

Jack took a sip of his liquorice tea and grimaced.

'You look like you're enjoying that,' said Bob.

'It's good for your iron levels,' said Jack.

Bob lifted his coffee mug to his face and rested his right cheek against its warmth. He held it there for a few seconds and then pulled it away. I'd seen him do it before. I assumed it was a comfort thing. 'How's things with you, Freddie?' he said. 'Don't know how you cope in that house with all those cats. It'd drive me mad.'

'He manages,' said Jack.

I put my mug on the coffee table, stood up and walked over to the bay window. It had started to drizzle with rain. I could hear Jack and Bob chatting behind me. They seemed to be getting on better than ever. Jack was saying he had a cupboard full of gluten free food; Bob said he only smoked menthol cigarettes to clear his sinuses.

'You okay, Freddie?' said Jack.

'I'm fine,' I said.

*Freddie – January 2014*

I went with Bob to visit Terry in the care home.

A member of staff met us in the reception area, told us her name was Angela. She wore a navy blue trouser suit uniform with a white badge pinned to the smock top. The badge said Key Worker.

'Follow me,' she said.

'I know the way,' said Bob.

'We have to escort you, sir. Health and safety.'

We followed her in silence down a never ending corridor with spillage proof flooring and wipe easy walls. There was a pervading smell of bleach and stale breath. It felt like the sort of route that needed a mortuary as its end point. We walked past closed and open bedroom doors, some with black and white pictures of residents blue-tacked on the oak veneer. The pictures had all been taken in the reception area. No-one was smiling. Occasionally we walked past a room with a television on, Noel Edmonds opening boxes on Deal or No Deal.

Angela stopped outside bedroom number twenty-eight.

'Here we are,' she said.

'I know,' said Bob.

We opened the door and walked into the bedroom.

Terry was sitting in a chair by the window, a restraining belt fixed tightly around his waist, his glassy eyes staring vacantly around the room. Gloopy streams of saliva dripped from his mouth, soaking into his food-stained lumberjack shirt and black tracksuit bottoms. He looked wedged in the chair, like someone had dropped him from a great height.

'The chair keeps him safe,' said Bob. 'He falls if he tries to stand.'

'Hello, Terry,' I said, sitting down on the bed and taking his hand. I felt a tiny amount of pressure returned, which made me feel desperately sad.

'He squeezed my hand,' I said.

Bob knelt down in front of the chair and wiped Terry's mouth with a paper tissue. 'It's the only way we know you're in there, isn't it, old friend?' He threw the tissue in the waste paper bin and took Terry's other hand.

*Jo-Jo – July 2015*

---

I found Amy in the far corner of the hotel conservatory. She was standing next to a Yucca tree, her iPhone pressed to her ear. She put up her hand. I walked over and sat down in one of the cottage suite chairs. I could only hear her side of the conversation, but it was obvious she was talking to Dan.

'Were you in bed?'

'Oh, it was just something Mum said. Made me feel a bit guilty.'

She held the phone closer to her mouth.

'She's not said much, but I think she really cares about him.'

'What's that mean?'

'Well, it's better than being Mr Fate Will Decide.'

She turned back towards me and raised her eyebrows.

'I know. I'll be back next week.'

'Yeah, Mum's coming with me.'

She faced the window.

'You liar. I bet you're sprawled over my side.'

'Ditto.'


## Jo-Jo – May 1980

Blackpool. I'd convinced Freddie to swap Springsteen for Michael Jackson's 'Off the Wall'. Three weeks earlier we'd camped out in my lounge and I'd made him listen to the whole album – two o'clock in the morning curled up on the floor under a duvet, drinking tea and eating thick cut toast covered in marmite.

Freddie stroked the steering wheel of the Avenger like it was the most sumptuous fur he'd ever come across, his chipped front tooth beaming out through the joyous grin super glued to his face.

'It's wonderful,' I said. 'I feel like I'm on the Monte Carlo rally. I'm going to get our names across the windscreen, some cuddly toys on the back seat.'

He squeezed my thigh. We raced past a motorway service station.

'Are we stopping soon?'

He shook his head. 'I want to get booked in early.'

'Suits me,' I said. 'We can go and look at the sea.'

'I want it to be perfect,' he said.

I put my hand on top of his, which was resting idly on the gear stick. I turned back towards the open window, the wind blowing in my face; the M6 streaming by at seventy miles per hour.

***

It took us an hour to find the street and another twenty minutes to find a place to park. We stood on the pavement looking up at the semi-detached house of the Bed and Breakfast.

'There must be somewhere better down by the front,' said Freddie.

'Let's at least have a look inside.'

'Let's not. We're miles from the sea.'

I started to walk up the driveway. 'I'm going to have a look,' I said.

'Okay,' he said, holding up his hands and following me.

We walked across the crumbling tarmac and reached the flaking red paint of the front door. I rang the bell. 'There's no place like home' chimed out of the tiny speaker.

'You can say that again,' said Freddie.

We laughed.

I looked at the neighbouring houses. 'It does look a bit rough round here.'

Freddie dropped on one knee, took hold of my hand and gazed up at me. 'I'll protect you,' he said. 'No-one messes with the woman of an Avenger driver.'

I slapped his arm. 'Idiot. Get up. People might be watching.'

He stood up and pulled me close. 'Try the bell again,' he said, nodding towards the front door.

I pressed the button a second time. There was still no reply.

'This is definitely it,' he said, fumbling in his back pocket and pulling out a crumpled letter. 'Look. It's this address. Three nights booking confirmed.'

I double checked. It all tallied. I pressed the bell for a third time, this time keeping my finger on the button.

'All right, all right, I'm coming. Give me a chance.'

The front door opened, but it caught on a safety chain. A bald-headed man stared out at us. 'Yes,' he said. 'What do you want?'

'Mr Lewis?' said Freddie.

'Yes.'

'We've got a room booked. Mr and Mrs Charlton.'

The man mumbled something and we heard the chain drop out of its catch. The front door opened wide. 'Come in. Come in,' he said, standing to one side and ushering us over the threshold. He had owl-like eyes and a mile-wide toothy grin.

'We'd like to see the room,' I said.

He looked behind us. 'Where are your cases?'

'In the car. But we want to see the room before deciding whether to stay.'

'Not stay?'

'Well, you are quite a way from the sea.'

'It's a five-minute walk through the back garden,' said Mr Lewis. 'You'll pay twice as much near the front. And you'll be lucky to get anything this week, with the weather being so nice.'

'We'd still like to see the room.'

He sighed and started to limp up the stairs, holding the bottom of his back. 'Okay,' he said. 'Follow me.'

'You all right?' said Freddie.

'Oh, don't worry about me, son. It's just me arthritis in me back... and me knees... and me hip...'

Freddie grinned at me and I sniggered. Mr Lewis looked back at us. 'You really named Charlton?'

'Yes,' said Freddie. 'What are you suggesting?'

'Nothing, son,' he said, turning away and resuming his limp up the stairs. 'It's just, you'd be surprised how many of the World Cup team I get stay here. Mr and Mrs Hurst; Mr and Mrs Moore. They've stayed twice this year.'

We laughed.

He faced us again. 'How old are you two?'

'Old enough to pay your rent,' I said.

Thirty minutes later Freddie came panting back into the attic room. 'Do you know how many stairs there are in this place?' he said, dropping the bags on the floor and flopping down on the bed.

I looked at him quizzically from the window. 'Why would I know that?'

'The answer is too many, especially when I'm carrying that bloody carpet thing of yours. What have you got in it? We're only here for three nights.'

'Woman stuff. Stop moaning and come and look at the view. You can see the sea from here.'

He groaned, dragged himself off the bed and walked over to the window. 'Where?' he said.

I pointed at the horizon. 'Over there.'

'That's just the sky.'

'No. Look. It's the sea.'

'It can't be,' he said. 'This room's facing the wrong way. I think the sea's behind us.'

'No. It's definitely the sea,' I said.


*Jo-Jo – July 2015*

---

Amy closed her phone, walked over to the cottage chairs and sat down. 'I told you he never goes to bed before two,' she said.

I smiled. 'How are the kids?'

'Sophia's had another row with her boyfriend, says she hates him.'

'They'll make up.'

'Maybe. Dan says she's been staring at her phone all day.'

A waitress came over, carrying a silver tray. 'Cream tea,' she said. 'I've charged it to your room.'

Amy pointed at the small coffee table between the two chairs. 'I shouldn't really,' she said. 'It's my second this week. Did you want something, Mum?'

I shook my head. The waitress put the tray on the table and walked away in the direction of the restaurant.

Amy spread a scone with strawberry jam. 'They're freshly baked you know, Mum. And the jam's homemade. You should try one.'

I looked out of the conservatory window. I could see the car park and its surrounding border of neatly pruned conifers. I scanned my eyes across the line of parked cars and felt a sense of relief when I saw the Mazda. I wondered whether to mention the ditto line from Amy's telephone conversation with Dan. I'd told her so many times. 'I thought you were meant to be a die-hard romantic. Tell him you love him.' I always got the same response. 'Mind your own business, Mum. He knows what ditto means.'

'You okay,' said Amy. 'You look a bit flushed. I thought you were having a lie down.'

'Freddie phoned,' I said. 'He wants me to call him back.'

'That's great,' she said, licking a blob of clotted cream off her finger. 'I told you he would. So why the anxious face? Oh, Mum, if you're worried about Dad, it's been two years. He'd have been happy for you.'

'It's nothing to do with your father.'

'What then?'

'It's just… well, perhaps it's best to leave the past where it belongs.'

'You're only going for a meal.'

'It was always different with Freddie. I don't want to spoil the memory.'

'You think it'll still be the same, after all this time?'

'No, of course not.'

'I never really understood why you wanted to look for him in the first place.'

'Curiosity,' I said. 'Ghosts. Thinking about what might have been…something.'

'Mum. It's a meal. You don't have to sleep with him.' She held out her phone. 'Call him,' she said.

## Freddie – July 2015

When I was twelve, I wrote my list of the ten best ways to commit suicide. It was all Fat Nigel's fault. He was in our class at school and nearly starved himself to death, went down to four and a half stone, had to be put on a drip. No one noticed. He must have been throwing his food away for weeks, but he carried on wearing the same size clothes. Everyone, including the teachers, carried on calling him Fat Nigel.

Jack tried to help with the list. 'What about shooting yourself? Or hanging. Hanging would be good.'

'Where would you get a gun, Jack?'

'Do you know how to tie a knot?'

We used to dare each other to stand right at the edge of the kerb as the bus raced past. He always stepped back, but I stayed absolutely still, the wind making me gasp for breath. When Dave Cooper moved into a flat on the thirteenth floor we used to visit him just to look out at the world from his balcony. I'd stand out there talking to them through the open French door. 'It'd be like flying if you jumped from here. Come and have a look.'

I thought about going back to the coffee shop from Jack's, but decided to go home instead. Under Jack's supervision, I'd called Jo-Jo's number and left a message with the hotel receptionist. The only thing I could do now was wait for her to call back. Maybe she wouldn't call. Maybe I wouldn't have to worry about meeting her again. I still couldn't work out why she'd wanted to find me in the first place.

I walked into my street and felt the usual sense of urgency to get inside the house. I wanted to break into a run. I needed to find out if everything was exactly as I'd left it. Perhaps I'd left the gas on or the taps running; perhaps I hadn't locked the door properly; maybe there'd been a break in. I forced myself to get my keys slowly out of my pocket, trying all the time to remember that people were watching.

*Freddie –April 1970*

---

Jack and I were sitting on top of my dad's whitewashed gates pitching conkers at each other. Dad had shown me how to soak the conkers in vinegar and bake them in the oven, said it would make them indestructible.

'Strings,' shouted Jack as the conkers tangled together.

I inspected my conker – the insides were peeping out through a split across its centre. 'It's busted,' I said.

'Hold it up,' he said. 'I get another go. That's the game.'

I hung my conker out, my whole body stiffening up. I wondered what had gone wrong with Dad's plan.

Crack.

'That makes mine a six-er,' he said.

'You were lucky,' I said, picking bits of conker from the grubby string. 'Come on, let's get the ball, they'll be here soon.'

We jumped down from the gate.

'My mum says your dad's dead,' he said, kicking a stone into the road.

I shrugged and ran up my path to fetch the Casey ball from the shed.

*Freddie – November 1972*

---

My mum was eighteen when she married my dad – a proper man she called him. I never heard her shout, but she could sulk for England. I fell in a pond on a day trip when I was five. Dad pulled me out in seconds, but Mum wrapped me in a blanket, packed up the picnic and made him take us home. She didn't speak to him for weeks. 'How's it my fault?' he said, but she just looked at him as if it was the stupidest question she'd ever heard. I've got a picture of Mum scowling at the camera on a day trip to London. Dad used to get the picture out every so often. 'Here's your mother enjoying herself,' he'd say. She cooked, knitted and sewed her way through life. Bread and butter puddings, egg custards, steak and kidney pies. She knitted Dad a green jumper. It stretched in the wash, the arms touching the floor when she hung it on the line. 'You're ruining that kid,' Dad would say every time I sat on her lap. She'd pull me close and glare at him.

Mum had placed her emergency candles around the lounge. 'Bloody strikes,' she said. 'Put some coal on the fire, son.'

I jumped off the settee and walked over to the bucket at the side of the hearth.

'Not too much.'

'I know, Mum. Two big lumps at the back and the little ones at the front.'

I watched as she walked around the room. She was striking matches from a Swan Vesta box and lighting her candles. It reminded me of Dad trying to light his pipe, holding a match to his Old Holborn tobacco and puff, puff, puffing away; the veins on his forearms throbbing out through his anchor tattoos from his merchant navy days. Mum walked over to our oak veneered sideboard, which she'd had since her wedding day, and lit one of the candles next to Dad's pink dish. It had a dancing nymph statue as its centrepiece. 'That's his guilt dish,' she'd tell everyone. 'Bought it after he'd been out drinking with his mates.'

She caught me looking at her and smiled. 'You're a good boy,' she said.

I flopped on the carpet in front of the fire, listening to the slack as it crackled away, watching the yellow and blue flames being pulled up the chimney. The warmth felt as though it was burning my cheeks. Dad's porcelain dogs looked down on me from the mantelpiece. Mum came and sat next to me. She touched my face.

'You okay, Freddie? You warm enough?'

I nodded.

'Brush my hair,' she said, holding out a blue plastic hairbrush.

I knelt behind her and she pulled out her tightly pinned hairclips. She shook her head. Her jet black hair tumbled down her back and I brushed.

'That's nice,' she said. 'Your dad used to do this for me.'


*Freddie – June 1970*

---

I ran across the damp grass and crossed the ball to Jack. He headed it back to one of the kids from the next estate who toe punted it past the goalie. We all jumped on the scorer and hugged him.

Rob, who lived three doors away from me, fetched the ball from Mr Perry's hedge. 'It's burst,' he said. 'Where'd you get it? It's crap.'

'I think Mum got it from the market.'

'Tell her to get us another one.'

'I'll ask her tonight,' I said.

He stepped towards me and pushed me in the chest. 'Tell her now. Go on. Go now.' He looked around at the other lads and then back at me. 'You're a Mummy's Boy,' he said. 'Your dad's dead and you're a Mummy's Boy.' He started clapping. 'Mummy's Boy. Mummy's Boy,' he chanted. He turned back to the others, encouraging them to join in. They all circled me, pushing me backwards and forwards; wide eyes and stupid grins leering at me. I looked for Jack. 'He's not going to help you. No one helps a Mummy's Boy.' Someone pushed me from behind. I swung round and threw a punch. It missed. Rob laughed and crashed his fist into my nose. I fell to the ground, face down on the grass.

'Get up, Mummy's Boy. Get up and fight.'

'Freddie! Freddie! Your tea's done.'

'Mummy's calling you, Mummy's Boy. Off you go for your tea.'

I wiped my face with the back of my hand. Tears, blood and snot smeared across my cheek.

*Freddie – July 2015*

---

As I put my key in the lock, I wondered if I should have stayed at Jack's. My head felt like it was full of syrup, milky floaters were swimming across my vision. I was sweating and shivering at the same time. I closed my front door, walked into the kitchen and got a bottle of water from the fridge. I poured some of the water into a glass, took four of my beta-blockers and sat down at the kitchen table, waiting for the drugs to take effect.

I didn't take the beta-blockers every day, they were there more as a comfort blanket, but I still cashed the script every month, stockpiling the surplus. I had a year's supply stored away in a battered copper chest, which I kept in the loft. My stash. My exit plan. I'd sit up there in an evening and count out the button size purple tablets, trying to work out how many it would take. My plan was to tip them all into a bucket and push handfuls at a time into my mouth, taking swigs of Vodka to wash them down.

The phone rang. I answered it on the second ring.

'Hello.'

'Freddie. It's Jo-Jo.'

'Jo-Jo. How are you?'

'I'm okay. Not changed much since you saw me this morning.'

'Sorry. I meant, did you get back okay?'

'Is that why you called?'

'What?'

'To ask me if I'd got back okay.'

'No. I…Where are you staying?'

'About ten miles away from where I left you.'

Silence.

'Are you still there, Freddie?'

'I didn't call to see if you'd got back okay.'

'No?'

'I wanted to check that as well of course.'

'That's good. And we've established that I did.'

A voice inside my head was saying, 'Ask her. Ask her. Ask her.' I still couldn't believe I was talking to her.

'I would like to meet up. If you meant it.'

'Why wouldn't I have meant it?'

I felt my cheeks flush again. 'It's what people say, isn't it?'

'I meant it,' she said.

***

I looked at the bedside clock. 4.00 A.M. Tai, my little black cat, was snoring away on the vacant side of my double bed. I was massaging her head, which always sent her into a deep sleep. Jo-Jo. The meal. Tonight. What would we talk about? The coffee shop was different. I hadn't known she was coming, hadn't had time to think. She'd given me the photo. She'd told me about her family. Maybe I should phone her and say I couldn't make it. I turned over and punched the pillow. Tai opened her one eye. Jack was right. I could be such a wanker.

## Jo-Jo – July 2015

A couple we saw at dinner the previous evening came into the conservatory. They stood out because of their difference in height, him over six foot with a bushy grey beard and a cap that made him look the spitting image of Captain Birdseye; her a foot shorter, with a stooped gait that made her look even smaller. They were holding hands as always. I'd told Amy off for saying they looked like a ventriloquist and his dummy on a works outing. We'd nicknamed them Hansel and Gretel. People watching was good, but giving them fictional names made it more fun. They looked over and caught me staring. I handed Amy back her iPhone.

'That seemed like hard work, Mum.'

'Yes,' I said.

'He is okay isn't he?'

'What do you mean?'

'You know, mentally?'

'He's shy, Amy. That doesn't make him mad.'

'I'm just saying, you haven't seen him for years. You never really told me why you split up.'

'It got complicated. Where's that waitress? I could do with a cup of tea.'

'Complicated in what way?'

'University started. I went away. We lost touch.'

'But if you felt so strongly about each other?'

'It wasn't that simple.'

'Why?'

'The distance for a start.'

'I thought you went to Lincoln.'

'I did.'

'Right.'

'What?'

'Well, it's not that far.'

'It wasn't just that.'

The waitress reappeared.

I called her over and ordered a pot of Earl Grey.

Freddie was sitting in the wicker chair and I was lying on my single bed underneath a poster of Starsky and Hutch. They were pretending to arm wrestle across the bonnet of Starsky's cherry-red Ford Gran Torino. It had large white vector stripes on either side, the striped tomato Hutch called it.

'We would like to offer you an unconditional place… Can you believe that, Freddie?'

'Great,' he said.

I patted the bed. 'Come and give me a cuddle.'

He walked over and lay down next to me.

'Tell me you're happy for me,' I said.

'Lincoln,' he said. 'It's so far away.'

'It's only for three years. And there's the holidays. We can write, talk on the phone. You can visit. It'll fly by.'

'I'm not good at writing.'

'It'll be good practice for you then.'

'It won't be the same.'

'I know, but I have to do this.'

'We've only just started, Jo-Jo.'

'And this needn't get in the way. It'll be different, exciting.'

'You'll soon forget about me.'

'For God's sake, Freddie. It's Lincoln.'

*Jo-Jo – July 2015*

'Look, Mum, if you don't want to tell me why you split up, that's fine.'

'There wasn't really a reason. We just drifted apart.'

'So when did you last see him?'

'Before I went to university.'

'And that was it?'

I nodded.

'He didn't call you?'

'No. He didn't call me.'

'I thought he loved you.'

## Jo-Jo – September 1980

I was in the outdoor of the Saddler's Arms. We used to go in there every Friday night to buy microwaved steak and kidney pies and bottles of Vimto, taking them back to my house to watch 'Pot Black' with my dad. The old woman, Elsie, was in her usual spot at the oak panelled bar, staring at the froth in her half pint of stout like it contained the secrets of the universe. Tony Kelly, the leather clad biker bully, was standing by the cigarette machine, nursing a pint of Bank's mild. He used to ride around the estate on his Kawasaki motor bike, looking for school kids to torment. If he found any, he'd fire a catapult of his dad's fishing maggots at them and then ride away laughing. He asked me out once and then spat at me when I said no. He looked up from his beer. I turned my back and leaned closer into the payphone receiver. Freddie's voice said 'hello' and then I heard the pips. I pushed a two pence piece into the slot.

'It's me,' I said.

'Have you phoned them?'

He made his question sound urgent, like it was the only thing that mattered.

'No, Freddie. You know I haven't. I told you last night.'

Silence.

'Are you not going to talk to me?'

'I don't want you to go,' he said.

'I want to. It's all arranged.'

'You could go next year.'

'Let's not do this again. I'm going next week.'

Silence.

'I've got no more money, Freddie. Are you coming round?'


Jo-Jo – July 2015

---

'Oh my God,' said Amy. 'I've just realised.'

'Realised what?' I said.

'You don't know? That's why you're not saying. He said he'd call you and he didn't. Why didn't you call him?'

I sat back in the chair and crossed my legs. 'It was all a long time ago. It doesn't matter now.'

'Pride,' she said. 'That's it. Isn't it?'

'And I suppose you'd have called Dan?'

'Probably not.'

'Definitely not,' I said.

'Is that why you wanted to see him? To find out why?'

'Partly.'

'Been the first thing I'd have said to him. Depending on his answer, it might have been the last.'

'It wasn't the only reason.'

'You still love him, don't you?'

She reached across the table and squeezed both my hands. She had tears in her eyes. 'Oh, sweetheart,' I said. 'What's wrong? It's okay. I'm just being silly. A silly old fool.'

She looked up at me. 'If you tell Dan about me crying, I will assassinate you.'

I laughed.

'I'm not joking,' she said.

I hugged her again. 'I know, my darling. I know.'

*\*\*\**

The beach was deserted as I walked along the shoreline hand in hand with Dad.

A black mass of cloud anchored itself on the horizon. Something burst out from its centre and flew towards us.

'What is it, Dad?'

'It's a dragon, sweetheart.'

The creature reached the beach and hovered above our heads. I could see its fleshy underbelly and green spiky back scales, fitting together like intricate jigsaw pieces.

'Dragons aren't real, Dad.'

'This one is.'

The dragon landed with a thud on the sand, making me drop my ice-cream. It had red puckered lips and long black mascaraed lashes sitting on top of award winning come-to-bed eyes. Dad let go of my hand, walked over and climbed on its back.

'Come back, Dad,' I shouted, but he ignored me, leaned over and whispered something in the dragon's ear.

The dragon laughed and flew off in the direction of the clouds.

My eyes flashed open.

Daylight was streaming across the bed through a crack in the hotel curtains, 4.00 A.M. flashing at me from the bedside clock. I looked again at the Lowry. Suit man was still staring out to sea, the dogs waiting patiently behind him.

Freddie.

I was eighteen, leaving home, leaving Dad, and Freddie's seal-pup eyes were looking up at me, waiting for me to decide, waiting for me to tell him it was all going to be okay. I asked him once why he loved me. 'It's obvious,' he said. And to him it was. He'd placed me on a sky-scraper pedestal like I was the brightest, most talented star in a billion dollar Broadway show

– that's how he made me feel. He was the man who promised to phone, the man who hadn't held me for long enough in the coffee shop, the man who'd stayed rooted in my head from the moment Debbie Harry had brought him into my life. I'd tried to explain the attraction to Amy, but it had come out all wrong, made him sound desperate, needy. Maybe he was. Maybe I was.

*Freddie – July 2015*

I drove Jack's Mini Cooper to the hotel, Mum occupying my thoughts.

My mum grieved Dad's death for the rest of her life, but she did have her 'friend', George – a short fat man in a brown, shiny suit who was a foreman at the factory where she worked. The first time I saw him he pulled up outside our house in his battered green Simca. All the kids from the street laughed, Rob shouted 'baggy arse' at him and Jack's brothers egged and floured his car.

George would take Mum to the Working Men's Club, where she'd have a bitter lemon and a game of bingo with her brothers. I'd lie in bed listening to him asking her for a goodnight kiss. 'You can go now,' she'd say, and he'd shuffle off back to his bedsit. When he finally made it inside our house, Mum used to make him sit in the chair by the window – 'no sense in ruining all the chairs, the way you fidget' – and she'd tut at him every time he crossed his legs. Sometimes she'd fall out with him and he wouldn't visit for weeks. I'd look out of the bedroom window and she'd be standing at the bus stop with her bag, frowning because God knows who would sit by her. She never gave in though. Reconciliation was always on her terms.

George stayed in our lives for twenty-five years. He had a heart attack after he retired from work and we heard he'd taken to his bed, one of the women in his block of flats looking after him. I asked Mum why she didn't visit. 'What's it got to do with me?' she said.

The table at the hotel was booked for seven-thirty, but I wanted to get there early and find somewhere to park. The car was two months old and still had that new car smell. Jack had bought it as a reward for passing his Best Interest Assessor course. A yellow Mickey Mouse air freshener, hanging from one of the vents, bounced against the dashboard as I rolled carefully over the speed bumps on the outskirts of the village. A few spots of rain fell on the windscreen, triggering the automatic wipers, saving my desperate search for the right switch or lever. 'Had I locked the front door?' landed as a thought inside my head. I took a deep breath and told myself to relax, the hypnotic swish, swish, swish of the wipers helping me to calm down.

*Freddie – May 1980*

---

I'd worked out the quickest route to the sea front and we'd run Mr Lewis' five minute walk in a ten minute jog. We made our way down the nearest set of steps and along the beach to a sheltered spot not far from the pier. Jo-Jo stepped out of her pink Crocs and crunched her toes into the malted-milk-coloured sand. She unrolled two Charlie Brown beach towels and handed one to me. We laid them out on the beach, side by side. I took off my Adidas t-shirt and put on my Foster Grant sunglasses. Jo-Jo frowned at me.

'What?'

'They're huge,' she said. 'They make you look old, like you're trying to hide the bags.'

'I like them.'

'Yeah, but you've got no taste, Freddie. The John Lennon ones are in my carpet bag. We'll bring those tomorrow.'

I straightened out the edges of my towel and lay down. Grains of sand itched against my back. I looked up at the walkway. A row of people were standing above us eating 99 ice creams or staring out at the horizon through the penny a go telescopes. I could hear 'Teddy Bears' Picnic' tinkling out of a rocking yellow play bus, a little girl yanking hard at its steering wheel, giggling with excitement, her mother standing to the side, smiling encouragement. Ted and Alison, a couple from our B and B, were leaning on the green metal railings and looking down at us. They waved. I waved back. Ted said something to Alison.

'They come from Walsall,' said Jo-Jo, sitting down on her towel. 'Just up the road from us.'

'Yeah.'

'Don't you think that's odd?'

'What?'

'Living so close and ending up in the same B and B.'

'Not really.'

'It's fate,' she said.

'You don't believe in that stuff, do you?'

'Don't you?'

'Why would we be destined to meet them?'

'We don't know yet, Freddie. That's how it works.'

*\*\**

We skipped Mr Lewis' cod and chips tea and found one of the restaurants on my list. Jo-Jo declared Malibu and ice as our drink for the evening – 'No-one gets drunk on Malibu,' she said. Three hours later we did the 'I'm not drunk' walk out of the bar.

It was past midnight when we got back to the B and B. I closed the front door behind us. A Tiffany shade table lamp lit up the hallway and a second lamp lit up the landing, guiding the route to our bedroom. Jo-Jo stood on the first step of the stairs and pulled me towards her.

'I told you he was nice,' she said. 'He's left the lights on for us.'

'Come on,' I said. 'Let's go to bed.'

'I want you to carry me.'

'There's no way I'm carrying you up those stairs.'

'If you love me, you will.'

I looked up at the landing.

'It's not that far,' she said. 'Not for a big, strong man like you.'

'You're really drunk, aren't you?'

'Yes,' she said, closing her eyes and nodding. 'I'm really drunk.'

I lifted her in my arms and started to walk up the stairs. She put her finger to her lips and made a shushing noise. I tripped up a step and she laughed. 'Quiet, Mr Charlton,' she said. 'Someone will hear us.'

One of the bedroom doors opened and Alison peered down at us over the bannister. She was wearing a pink flannelette dressing gown and holding a Ruth Rendell novel. Ted appeared next to her in his paisley pyjamas. 'What's going on?' he said. 'Oh, hello. Are you two okay?'

Jo-Jo stroked my cheek. 'He's my hero,' she said.

\*\*\*

We'd made it to the bed. I was awake. Jo-Jo was asleep.

I kissed her forehead. She muttered something and turned over, the back of her head now facing me. I sniffed her hair. It smelt of strawberry shampoo. She pulled the white Egyptian cotton sheet up around her shoulders. I'd pushed the sheets and blanket back on my side, but Jo-Jo had kept herself covered, said it made her feel safe. She muttered something else. It sounded like peas. I smiled and thought about what she'd said on the beach, about fate, about Ted and Alison. I couldn't think of a single thing we had in common with them. Ted wore a brown corduroy jacket with leather patches on each elbow and Alison laughed like a hyena at everything he said. I pulled Jo-Jo into my body and squeezed her close.

*****

We were in a wood, walking hand in hand. I could hear birdsong, Elvis Costello singing 'Alison'. And then we were in the middle of town, standing outside Midland Educational, still holding hands. I could hear pigeons cooing. It sounded like they were calling over and over, 'do it now, do it now; do it now.' Someone pinched the end of my nose. I opened one eye. Jo-Jo was smiling at me.

'Your turn to make the tea,' she said.

'In a minute,' I said, turning over.

She kissed the back of my neck. I turned back towards her.

'I'm thirsty,' she said.

'I'm not surprised.'

'You shouldn't let me drink so much.'

She put her head on my chest and pulled at my chest hairs. I could feel her warm skin through her silk nightdress, her bare thighs touching mine. She slid her hand across my stomach and under the waistband of my boxer shorts.

'I thought you were tired,' she said.

*Freddie – August 1980*

---

Jo-Jo's bedroom, cuddling up on her single bed. Her mum and dad out shopping, Josh in his room, listening to his latest Genesis album.

'Let's get married,' I said.

'I'm not ready for that, Freddie.'

'We're good together. I'll find a vicar, someone we can talk to.'

'Not yet.'

'Why? I love you.'

'I know.'

'But you're still going?'

'It's three years. And it's Lincoln. If it's real, we'll survive.'

'Do you love me?'

'What?'

'You've never said you love me.'

'I struggle with that. You know I do.'

'Maybe that's the problem. All that stuff with your dad.'

'Maybe the problem is you want it too much.'

'What?'

'You. It's all about you. I know your mum's—'

'—It's nothing to do with my mum.'


*Freddie – July 2015*

---

I could see the diners through the Mini's rain splattered windscreen. They were gathered in the hotel's conservatory, a yellow glow from the central chandelier enveloping them like a protective cloak. Two couples were sitting in wicker chairs, a bottle of wine in an ice bucket placed in the centre of their tables; further along, a man, a woman and two children, and, at the table next to them, an older couple, the man reading a broadsheet, the woman looking in her handbag.

I unfastened my seatbelt. The Mini's engine was still running. It had taken me four or five goes to park evenly between the white lines, equidistant on each side of the car.

A knock on the passenger side window made me jump.

There was a pocked faced, moustachioed man staring in at me. He was wearing a high visibility jacket and a black cap with Security Guard written across the front in yellow letters. He gestured for me to wind the window down. I pressed a switch on the dashboard, opening the window by about six inches.

'Are you staying in the hotel, sir?'

'No. I'm here to meet a friend. We're having dinner.'

'Ah, you'll need to move the car then. This area's for hotel guests only. The restaurant parking's on the other side.'

He gestured to the far side of the car park, no more than a hundred metres away.

I nodded and pressed the switch again, closing the window.

I watched him walk over to the three industrial size grey dustbins on the edge of the car park. He stood, hands on hips, watching me. He touched the peak of his cap and pointed again towards the non-resident parking spaces.


*Freddie – December 1980*

---

Yoko cremated John. I'd never heard of anyone being cremated. Mum told me it was pagan. I wrote to Yoko, told her I had a band, which I didn't, told her how John inspired us all, which he did. I cut the 'You may say I'm a dreamer...' quote out of Melody Maker, blue-tacking it on my bedroom wall; bought Double Fantasy, learned every word, and listened religiously to the Andy Peebles' interviews on a Sunday tea-time.

Forty-eight hours after the interview, Lennon was gone.

Mark Chapman shot him, but Yoko had him burned.

'Happy Christmas, John.'

'Happy Christmas, Yoko.'

I watched an episode of Cracker in which Robbie Coltrane's character, Fitz, was giving a lecture to a group of students. He was saying how everyone was waiting with impatience for their parents to die, waiting for a chance to move centre stage and suck up the grief, the attention, feel something, grasp at anything to break the mind numbing monotony of everyday life. He'd rehearsed the speech for his father's funeral for years, even got a bit irritated when his dad carried on living.

My mum expected to die in her own bed. She'd bought it with Dad when they got married and kept it for the rest of her life. The steel frame had to be bolted together with a special spanner and tied up with pieces of string at each corner.

She came home after her diagnosis. There were no clues it would end so quickly. She'd have her usual lie down in the afternoons, her 'turns' she called them – ever since Dad's death she'd had her turns. But the jaundice spread, covering her skin and filling the whites of her eyes. 'I've got the big C,' she told me, trying to sound like John Wayne – who my dad loved.

I was holding her hand when she died. She hadn't been conscious for a couple of days and her breathing had turned into a suck and blow rasp, which reverberated around the house. She'd inhale and then not exhale for a few seconds. I'd hold my breath and she'd start breathing again. I waited and waited after her last breath, squeezing her hand, staring at her mouth.

*Freddie's Requiem for Mum*

'My relationship with Mum was crafted through tragedy. My dad died when I was seven, leaving Mum to cope with raising a child whilst trying to recover from losing the man she loved and wanted to spend the rest of her life with. She survived, but only just, focussing all of her efforts on being a mum. She wouldn't allow anyone to criticise me: I had the bluest eyes, the best of looks and the highest form of intelligence. I could sort anything and everything – 'You'll sort it out,' she'd say, when most of the time I hadn't got a clue. Nothing fazed her and I found that confidence infectious.

She wasn't just my mum. She was a woman with hopes, dreams and ambitions, passionate in her love for my dad. I once asked her how she knew she was in love and she said my dad was always the first person she saw when she entered a room and, I'm guessing, the person she looked for when she left. Dad was Mum's life and a huge part of Mum died when he left her. She never found a way of dealing with her grief and life after my dad was about survival, nothing more.

Mum loved her siblings, telling us stories about growing up with them, like the time she worked in the pickled onion factory with her sisters, Theresa and Doris. She worshipped her dad and his wonderful lust for life. I never met my granddad but Mum used to make him come alive, telling us about his years as a publican, his singing, dancing, piano-playing, belly-laughing, soul of the party approach to living – the time his sons asked him what he was leaving them as an inheritance and he said, 'The world. Enjoy it. I have.' Every time she told the story she would laugh and that would make me laugh. She told her tales over and over, her face coming alive, wrinkling up, her mind a walking encyclopaedia of the family history, our connection with the past.

I'm not sure how I'll cope without Mum in the world and that is the saddest part for me. I'll miss her company. Perhaps one day I'll get a chance to see her again – I hope so. In the meantime, I hope you find Dad, Mum and, if he's half the man you thought he was, he'll be waiting for you with a big hug.'

Back on the beach, lying on the towels, me wearing Jo-Jo's sunglasses and tracking a fat brain-coloured cloud, willing it to crawl faster across the sky.

'He really loves Yoko,' I said.

'Who?'

'John Lennon. Who'd you think?'

'He calls her mother. That's just wrong.'

'It's a pet name.'

'It's weird. She controls him, even his love affairs.'

'What?'

'May Pang, that eighteen months lost weekend. Yoko arranged it all.'

'Shows how much she loves him.'

'Shows his weakness. A little boy. That's what he is.'

I touched the bridge of the sunglasses.

Jo-Jo sat up and ran her hand through her hair. 'A little, little boy,' she repeated.

I re-parked the car in one of the non-resident spaces, pulled on the handbrake and turned off the engine. I was facing towards the hotel's exit. I couldn't see the conservatory, but I could see the security man through the rear view mirror. He was still standing by the bins, still watching me.

I reached in the back seat for my jacket. For the first time in three years I was wearing my Jeff Banks' pin-striped suit that I'd bought second-hand off e-bay. The fastened up top button of my Van Heusen shirt was pinching at my throat. I undid the button, loosened my silk tie, took in a deep breath and looked out of the window. All of the conifers were slide-rule pruned, the lawns mowed and trimmed to perfection. We'd be having proper wine and food menus. I'd have to work out the knives and forks.

I thought about the coffee shop, about Jo-Jo turning up after all this time, all of our connections were three decades old. I wondered if she liked cats. A roll of anxiety turned in my stomach and I fumbled inside my jacket pocket for the strip of beta blockers that I'd brought with me.


*Jo-Jo – April 1981*

---

We stood in the front row of the church, waiting for Dad's coffin to be carried in by the top-hatted pallbearers, Mum staring straight ahead at a stained glass image of Christ in mid crucifixion, Josh and I each side of her, gripping her hands. Someone gasped. I turned my head and looked down the aisle. The procession was still stepping out towards us. I found out later that Uncle Arthur, Dad's eldest brother, had tripped himself up on the bottom of his new suit trousers. The coffin had slipped off his shoulder, but he'd caught it mid-fall and lifted it back in place without breaking his stride.

Josh found Dad in the back garden, but it was two months after the funeral before we talked about it.

'You never said what happened.'

'Not something I want to relive, Sis.'

'I'd still like to know, Josh.'

'I came home from college and there he was, face down on the lawn.'

'And he was already dead?'

'I think so.'

'Where was Mum?'

'In bed. She came down in her nightie, kept shaking him.'

The Student's Union, me eating the chilli special, Mr Averis, my dissertation supervisor, walking into the canteen, looking around, seeing me, bowing his head, coming over to my table, kneeling down in front of me, dandruff on his blue velvet sports jacket collar, patches of grey beard on his cheeks and under his nose.

'It's your father, Jo-Jo.'

'My father?'

'Shall we go somewhere more private?'

The church door creaked open. I turned and looked down the aisle.

Dad's woman from the park.


*Jo-Jo – May 1980*

---

We'd been sunbathing for two hours. I couldn't see Freddie's eyes behind the John Lennon sunglasses, but I knew he was asleep. A copy of Norman Mailer's 'The Naked and the Dead' lay open on his chest. It had a picture of a tin-hatted American soldier, holding a hand grenade and screaming something obscene out of a muddy trench. Jack had recommended the book, but I could see from the way it lay that Freddie had only managed to struggle through a couple of chapters before he'd nodded off. I yawned and sat up on my elbows. The beach was packed, but there was a free patch of sand directly in front of us. I pinched Freddie's arm.

'Wake up, lazy bones. I want you to build me a sand-castle.'

He lifted his sunglasses. 'A what?'

'A sand castle. You do know what a sand-castle is?'

He sat up and rubbed his eyes. The book slid off his chest. 'I wasn't asleep.'

'Yeah, right. I believe you.'

'What time is it?'

I reached into the beach bag for my watch. 'Twelve thirty.'

'Lunch-time,' said Freddie, dropping the glasses back over his eyes and lying back down on the towel.

I turned towards him and started curling the hairs on his chest. 'No lunch until I get my sand castle,' I said.

He looked at me. 'A sand castle?'

I nodded.

'What am I meant to build it with?'

I grinned and held up a yellow plastic bucket and spade set, still inside its red net bag. 'I bought it from the shop at the top of the steps,' I said. 'While you were asleep.'

'Okay. I'll build you a sand castle.'

'Four turrets,' I said. 'And don't forget the moat.'


*Jo-Jo – July 2015*

---

Mum had a photograph of Uncle Arthur, taken just before the war. He looks like a young Errol Flynn, with a pencil moustache. He used to drive around in highly waxed saloon cars with walnut dashboards and leather seats, taking Josh and me for rides in the country. I was frightened to move in case I dirtied anything. When they were teenagers, his brothers, including Dad, used to tease him when he wiped the pub seat with his white handkerchief before he sat down – 'Clean enough for you now, Arthur? Wouldn't want you catching anything.'

Arthur married twice. His first wife sold everything in the house and left him while he was away in India; his second wife, Peggy, had a stroke and he looked after her on his own for years, refusing any offer of help. He was seventy-three when he moved to Birmingham to live with another woman after Peggy died. But he kept his flat in Bloxwich – his bolt hole he called it.

I'd been at the table for ten minutes when I saw Freddie walking up to the reception desk. He said something to the receptionist who pointed towards the conservatory. Freddie turned, saw me, bowed his head for a split second and then looked at me again. I waved. He put his hands in his pockets and walked over to my table.

'Jo-Jo,' he said.

I noticed he was wearing thick framed, designer glasses, Joe 90 style. I didn't remember him having them on in the coffee shop. They looked good, accentuated his grey, blue eyes.

'I didn't think you'd come,' I said.

He ran his fingers through his hair. 'I nearly lost it in the car park.'

'Lost it?'

'I'm okay. It's just nerves.'

'Nothing to be nervous of.'

He sat down and swapped over his knives and forks.

I laughed. 'You still do that then?'

He gave me a puzzled look.

'With the cutlery, swap them over.'

'Oh, yes. Sorry. It's instinctive. Shall I put them back?'

'No. It's nice. Reassuring.'

The waitress came over.

'Would you like to see the wine menu?' she said.

Freddie and I smiled at each other.

*Jo-Jo – April 1981*

---

Dad carried on seeing his park woman, disappearing for evenings out with imaginary friends from his school days. No-one questioned him, except me. 'Leave it, Jo-Jo. I don't want to talk about it.' I used to watch him with Mum, looking for a change, waiting for his big announcement, convinced he'd leave us. There was no point relying on Mum. I was the eldest. I had to be ready. But he carried on being Dad. I wondered if he ever felt guilty, if he ever felt the need to tell her, to confess, to come clean. I wanted to tell her. I felt guilty. I felt dirtied by his grubby little secret. And then he died.

The vicar was over six feet tall, had a bulbous belly and a totally grey Brian Blessed beard. His voice boomed out to every corner of the church and everyone, even the children, went quiet when he stood up to start the service. 'How Great Thou Art,' my choice, was the first hymn. I couldn't take my eyes off Dad's coffin. It was light oak with a brass plaque in the centre of the lid. The thought that he was in there, listening to us, filled my head. The funeral director gave me and Josh a choice of coffins. We'd tried to get Mum involved, but she'd left it to us. 'Just get the one that's going to last him,' she'd said. 'And nice lining. It has to have nice lining.'

'Devoted husband... loving father... loved his garden...' The vicar said lots of nice words and we all walked serenely out of the church. 'They did him proud,' someone said. 'Nice sermon, Vicar,' another called out. Everyone offered their condolences to Mum, but she didn't answer. Josh thanked them. I looked for Dad's woman. I thought she'd gone and then I saw her, standing by the coffin, both hands resting on the lid. I looked at Mum, but she hadn't noticed. Josh had. He gave me a quizzical look. I shook my head. Mum and Josh walked outside. I walked back up the aisle.

'Hello,' I said.

'It wasn't just an affair, you know. We loved each other.'

She was staring at the coffin, looking as though she was talking to Dad. I didn't know what to say, how to react. I could see her hands were trembling. I expected her to burst into tears.

'You should be grateful for all the time you had with him,' she said.

And then she walked past me and out of the church.

I went up to the coffin and touched the lid. 'Goodbye, Dad,' I said.

## Jo-Jo – July 2015

I took a sip of the Muscadet. Freddie was still smiling at me.

'It's fine,' I said.

The waitress nodded and filled my glass. She turned to Freddie.

'I'll stick with water,' he said, pouring himself a drink from the jug in the centre of the table.

She nodded, put the bottle in the ice bucket and walked away towards the kitchen.

'Water?' I said.

'I never drink and drive,' he said.

'That sounds like one of your rules.'

'My rules?'

'You had rules for everything. Don't you remember?'

'I remember you always threatening to send the wine back.'

'I never did though.'

'No,' he said. 'I don't think you ever did.'

We picked up the food menus. The man at the next table had finished reading his newspaper. 'Where's that waitress?' the man said. 'I'm ready for my starter.' The woman with him looked around the restaurant.

'I know what you're having,' said Freddie.

'You do?' I said.

'Steak,' he declared, looking like a child who'd just got one over on the grown-ups. 'Rare, with the blood still running. I'm right aren't I?'

I could tell by the way he was looking at me how much energy his confidence had taken. I shook my head. It made me feel sad.

'You're not having steak?' he said.

'I'm vegetarian, Freddie. Have been for the last twenty years.'

*Jo-Jo – September 1980*

---

Digbeth Coach Station. Freddie and I were sitting on blue plastic seats at terminal twenty-four. I had my carpet bag on my lap and Dad's brown leather suitcase at my feet. The coach was parked in front of us.

I looked at my watch. 'He's cutting it fine,' I said.

'Still got five minutes,' said Freddie. 'Here he is now.'

The driver walked across the road from the canteen, an Express Coaches badge pinned to his jacket lapel. 'Morning,' he said, throwing the butt of his cigarette in the gutter. 'You two off to sunny Lincoln?'

'Just me,' I said, standing up and nodding at my suitcase. 'Can you store that one? I'll keep the bag with me.'

'No problem, Miss,' said the driver, touching his cap. He looked at Freddie and then back at me.

A man and a woman stood up from the plastic seats further along the concourse. The man picked up a suede holdall from the pavement and put it over his shoulder. He went to pick up a second holdall, but the driver, now holding my suitcase, rushed over. 'I'll get that for you, sir,' he said.

'Thank you,' said the woman, brushing down the back of her coat. 'Isn't that kind, Frank?'

The man nodded and, looking relieved, put the first holdall back on the floor. 'You couldn't take this one as well, could you?'

The driver opened up the luggage flaps on the side of the coach and pushed the bags inside. My suitcase went in first.

A younger couple, about the same age as me, each wearing a back pack, climbed the steps of the coach. 'You two going to Lincoln?' said the driver. 'That's right, mate,' said the girl, neither of them breaking stride as they ran laughing down the coach towards the back seat. The driver tutted at the older couple. 'Young love,' he said. 'I suppose they'll be giggling all the way.' He looked at me and then quickly went back to his bag duty.

'This is it then,' said Freddie.

'You should have come with me. I don't start until Monday. You could have helped me settle in.'

He shrugged. 'It's better this way.'

I pulled him towards me. 'I'll see you next week?'

He nodded. 'I'll book the Friday off and come up at the weekend.'

I kissed him on the lips. 'Stop looking so sad. It'll fly by.'

The driver, who was now sitting behind the steering wheel, started the engine. 'You coming, love?' he shouted.

I threw the carpet bag over my shoulder and kissed Freddie again. 'I'll see you soon. Don't forget to phone.'

'I promise,' he said.

I turned, climbed the steps and walked along to the middle of the coach. I put my bag in the overhead storage and sat down next to the window. Freddie put up his hand. He mouthed 'I love you' as the coach pulled away. I looked back, but he was already walking towards the exit, his hands in his pockets.

'Ob-la-di, Ob-la-da. Life goes on...'

I looked down the coach for the source of the singing. The back pack couple were now part of a group of six, three couples. One of the girls pulled a stack of multi-coloured plastic cups and a bottle of Bacardi out of a Marks and Spencer carrier bag. She gave the cups to the lad sitting next to her.

'Come on, Jess,' said the lad on the end. 'We're dying of thirst here.'

She unscrewed the cap on the Bacardi bottle and filled the cups, which the lad next to her was holding out one by one. With the cups half filled, he handed them round to the group.

I looked at the driver. He was watching the back seats in his rear view mirror.

'Excuse me.'

I looked up. There was a man standing in the aisle. He was wearing a navy blue Crombie coat and a black bowler hat, which he touched at the brim in greeting. I put his age at mid-thirties and, apart from the hat, the other striking thing about him was his Union Jack nose stud. I wondered why I hadn't seen him get on the coach.

'Do you mind if I sit here?' he said, tugging nervously at his two tone, mostly ginger but with patches of black, goatee beard.

I smiled. 'No,' I said.

He sat down. I realised I was staring at him and I turned to look out of the window.

'I was trying to read,' he said, waving a crumpled paperback book in my direction. 'But that song gets inside your head.'

I looked at his book: 'The Collected Works of Shelley.'

'My dad loves him,' I said.

'It's prep for my course,' he said.

'You're going to the University?'

'You sound surprised.'

'No, it's just, well—'

'— It's just, I'm a little old to be a student. Right?' He tapped the book. 'I want to study these guys before it's too late.'

'The rest of the guys in the band,' I said.

He looked at me quizzically.

'The Romantics. Shelley and the rest of the guys in the band. That's what my dad calls them.'

Dad learned Shelley's moonbeams and kisses poem off by heart, reciting it at every opportunity. I'd close my eyes and listen, entranced with the thought that you could love someone that much. I used to dream about Dad flying across a starry night sky on a magic carpet, searching for Mum, risking everything for a single kiss. I wanted to find my own Shelley. Dad met his woman in the park, but he stayed with Mum, sacrificed everything to look after her. Moonbeams and kisses versus loyalty and commitment. What a choice.

Josh married his first girlfriend, Glenda, who worked in a bank. He waited ten years before having his first child, had another the year after, and then no more. He'd paid off his mortgage by the time he was forty. Mum moved into a sheltered housing scheme after Dad died and Josh would phone her every night after Coronation Street or Heartbeat, depending on the day. Sometimes she'd ignore his call, getting it into her head it was a duty call. He'd phone back every half an hour until she answered. Every Sunday he'd take her to his house for lunch and they'd watch old westerns and Jimmy Cagney films – 'I'm on top of the world, Ma.' Some weeks she'd say she wasn't going, telling him on the Saturday night. 'Okay, Mum,' he'd say and then turn up the next day to pick her up. She was always ready.

One night, someone set fire to the landing in her block of flats. It was the middle of the night and Mum phoned my brother: 'Okay, Mum,' he said. 'I'm on my way.' He rang the fire brigade.

The starters arrived. Freddie had ordered the liver pate and I'd asked for the green salad. I was conscious of having sipped my way through my glass of wine. I wanted to refill the glass, but I fought the urge and poured myself a glass of water.

'It's okay,' he said. 'Don't feel you have to avoid the wine for me.'

'I'm not,' I said, a little too sharply. 'I'm thirsty.'

I carried on eating my salad. He put down his knife and then picked it up again. He looked as though he was going to say something, but he didn't. He looked at the table. I felt guilty for snapping.

'So, thirty-five years,' I said.

He was looking nervously around the room, wringing his hands, beads of sweat on his forehead. He took a drink of water, picked up his napkin and wiped his brow. 'It's warm in here,' he said.

'Are you okay, Freddie?'

'I'm fine.'

I forked some more salad into my mouth. The waitress came over and refilled my wine glass. I smiled at her. She walked back to the side of the conservatory, where she stood like a sentry on guard duty, surveying the room. I picked up the wine glass, took another drink, held the glass in front of me and swirled the Muscadet.

'Perhaps this was a mistake,' I said.

He pushed his half-eaten plate of pate away from him. 'I'm sorry. I don't do this very often.'

'Just relax. Tell me about Becky. How often do you see her?'

'I haven't seen her for twelve years, not since Mum died.'

I waited, but that was it. He was looking around the room again.

'You must miss her,' I said.

'Yes,' he said. 'She died really quickly. Nothing they could do.'

'I meant Becky,' I said.

***

I had trout for the main course. My vegetarianism didn't include fish, much to Jason's disgust. 'You can't pick and choose,' he used to say. 'Yes, I can, and I'm choosing to eat fish.'

Freddie had stopped sweating, which was just as well because he'd gone for the goat curry, but he was still clinging to his napkin, scrunching it up in his right hand. He kept touching the bridge of his glasses and pushing them back on his face. He told me about borrowing Jack's Mini for the evening, how he'd struggled to find the switch for the wipers. 'Typical, Jack,' he said. 'He just expects you to know everything.'

'Good of him to lend you the car, though.'

'Yeah, I had to sell my car when the job went.'

'When was that?'

'About a year ago.'

'So you haven't worked for a year?'

'I've been looking,' he said.

We both forked a mouthful of our food. I took a sip of wine.

'Do you remember the bear?' I said.

He looked at me.

'The one you won at the fair.'

I reached down, picked up my handbag, undid the zip and ceremoniously fetched out the six inches high teddy bear. I sat him in the middle of the table, leaning him against the water jug.

'You kept him,' he said.

'Yep,' I said. 'Carried him around all these years.'

Freddie picked up the bear and started to cry.

The waitress rushed over and asked if everything was all right. Freddie blew his nose into a napkin. The waitress and I averted our eyes. She asked if we wanted dessert. We said no and ordered coffee. She refilled my wine glass and walked away towards the kitchen. Freddie was still holding the bear.

'I didn't mean to upset you,' I said. 'I thought it would be nice.'

'It is,' he said. 'It's just, it's—'

The chipped tooth smile, the downcast eyes, the little boy

who'd stolen a toffee. He was back. For a split second my Freddie reappeared. I wanted to hug him. And then he was gone again.

'I'm sorry,' he said.

'Stop saying that,' I said.


*Jo-Jo's Dream*

---

I fist bang the front door.

'There's no-one here,' I shout.

'There must be,' she says.

I hit the door again and step back, looking up at the windows, waiting for a sign of life.

'He's gone,' I say, falling to my knees. 'He's gone.'

'No,' says Amy. 'He's here somewhere. We have to keep looking.'

Two nurses look at each other.

'She's twitching a lot. Do you think she can hear us?'

'They say she can, but she can't.'

'It makes you shiver doesn't it? Imagine being like that.'

'It's not natural, keeping her alive in that state.'

'The daughter sits for hours talking to her.'

'Poor cow. Let's get her changed.'

I lie there listening, screaming at them from inside my paralysed body. 'I'm here. I'm here. I'm here.'

We keep searching. I pull Amy down a jet-washed cobblestone road, passing a line of Victorian terraced houses, conifer lined driveways, lush green lawns, neatly trimmed privets, garden borders of rhododendron bushes and aphid free roses.

'This isn't right,' I say. 'He won't be here.'

'Where did you meet?' says Amy.

'What?'

'Try to think about him, Mum. It might help.'

The doctor's back. He's talking to Amy.

'The stroke was too severe, Mrs Graham. It's been six months now. There's no sign of any brain activity.'

'What about the twitching, doctor? I'm sure she knows I'm here.'

'Involuntary, I'm afraid. There's no conscious movement.'

'Are you sure?'

'As sure as we can be. Your Mum's not going to make any sort of recovery.'

'You mean, you want to turn off the machines?'

They do. Oh, my God. I need to find him. I need to find him now.

We carry on searching my head.

'This is hopeless,' I say.

'You can't give up, Mum.'

'What if he's not here?'

'He is. Tell me about his childhood. Where did he grow up? Did you visit?'

'Once.'

'Well?'

'It was so long ago.'

'Think. There must be something.'

'Yellow houses. I remember yellow houses.'

The nurses again.

'Matron told me they're going to switch off the machine tomorrow.'

'Sounds like the daughter's seen sense at last.'

'They should have done it weeks ago.'

'She seems a bit calmer today, less twitchy.'

We cross over the road and walk towards a circle of 1950s steel framed houses, all painted buttercup yellow. There's a play green in front of them with swings, a slide and make-shift goal posts. The smell of fish and chips and real coal fires lace the air.

'This is it,' I say.

'Which house?'

'I can't remember.'

She grabs my hand. 'Let's walk up and down until something clicks. Come on.'

We read the numbers as we walk: 46… 44… 42… I stop.

'What is it?' says Amy.

'There,' I say. 'The one with the Murano glass dogs in the window. We've found it.'

I can smell antiseptic wipes. They've already washed and changed me. Someone has switched on a radio. I can hear Chris Evans' breakfast show. I feel the nylon sheets being pulled back over my limp, helpless body, hear the door open, the footsteps of people walking towards the bed.

We look up at the house.

'I'm so scared,' I say.

'I know, Mum, but I'll be right here.'

I draw in a deep breath and walk up the driveway, the crunching gravel echoing inside my head. I reach the front door and single press the bell. The hallway light comes on. The door swings open. I look back at Amy.

'Are you ready, Mrs Graham?'

'Can you give me a minute, doctor?'

'Of course.'

I feel Amy's warm breath and moist lips touch my forehead.

'I hope I'm doing the right thing, Mum.'

No. Not yet. Not yet.

I'm inside the house, walking slowly down the hall, passing pictures of Freddie. School photographs, him wearing a sky blue uniform, shoulder length dark-black hair sticking out in all directions; the top two buttons of his shirt undone, his red check tie hanging loose in a wide knot.

I open the lounge door.

He's sitting on his Mum's brown leather settee, his chipped

front tooth smile beaming out at me. 'Hello, my darling. I've been waiting for you.'

I run over and hug him, his Kouros aftershave taking me back thirty-five years. I pull away, hold his face with both my hands and kiss him on the lips. 'Promise me you'll never leave me again. Promise me.'

'I promise,' he says, wiping tears from his face. 'I promise.'

## Jo-Jo – May 1980

Going home day. I'd sent Freddie off to fill the Avenger with petrol. He'd left me three twenty pound notes to pay Mr Lewis for our stay. I went downstairs, walked into the lounge area and found Alison sitting on one of the sofas. She was crying.

I rushed over and put my arm around her. 'What's happened?' I said.

She sniffed into a sodden paper tissue, which she'd curled up into a ball in her right hand. The tip of her nose had a red tinge. 'Ted's gone,' she said.

I pulled her closer. 'Have you had a row?'

She nodded and dabbed the end of her nose with the tissue. 'Last night,' she said. 'All I did was ask him to get the cases out of the wardrobe. He was watching some black and white film on the telly. You know what he said?'

I shook my head.

'In a minute. He's been saying it a lot lately. Everything's in a minute.'

She turned towards me, buried her face against my chest and sniffed into my new Adidas t-shirt. I gently eased her away.

'He'll be back,' I said.

'No,' she said, lifting her head. 'He won't. I told him he was a lazy pig, shouted at him. I don't know where it came from. It's such a stupid thing to fall out over. He said I was boring. That the only thing I thought about was my Tarot cards. It's not true. We do lots of things together. And then he slammed the door and left. All his stuff's still up there. He's taken the car.'

She put her head against my chest again. This time I let her stay.

'It's just a tiff,' I said, stroking her hair. 'It happens when couples go away together. Freddie and I are always falling out. '

'I don't know how I'm going to get home,' she said. 'All I asked him to do was get the cases out of the wardrobe.'

'It's okay,' I said. 'You can come back with us. He'll be waiting for you at home.'

She looked up at me with wide eyes like I'd suddenly rescued her from a burning building. 'Will he?' she said.

'Definitely,' I said, patting her leg. 'You just need a break from each other. Dry your eyes and fetch your bags.'

***

I tied the fluffy, yellow Snoopy to the interior mirror of the Avenger.

'Ah,' said Alison. 'He's sweet.'

She was sitting in the backseat and leaning through the gap in the front seats, talking to us, giving us the life and times of Ted and Alison: how they'd been together ten years, they didn't want any children; he was like a little boy really with his tantrums. She kept looking down and twisting the wooden buttons on her white Aran wool cardigan

'You mean he's left you like this before?'

'He's always doing it. Sulks for days sometimes.'

'Why do you put up with it?'

'It's just how he is,' she said.

I looked at Freddie, wanting him to say something. He was chewing hard on his bottom lip. I tried to work out if he was annoyed. He'd hardly spoken all the way home. I'd have understood if he'd been angry. I'd inflicted Alison on him.

'It's not far from here,' she said. 'Take the next right.'

We pulled up outside a three-storey block of flats. I got out of the car and pulled the front seat forward to let her out of the back. She hugged both of us. Freddie fetched her case from the boot and got back in the driver's seat. He'd left the engine running.

'The car's not here,' said Alison, looking nervously up at the flat. 'He's still sulking. It's what he does.' She nodded at the car. 'He didn't say much coming back.'

'He's fine,' I said.

She hugged me again, picked up her case and walked down the tarmac path. I got back in the Avenger, fastened my seatbelt and turned to wave, but she'd already gone through the entrance doors. Freddie u-turned the car and accelerated back towards the main road. Snoopy bounced against the window.

'He'd only do it once,' I said.

'You shouldn't get involved.'

'What was I meant to do? Leave her there.'

'I can't see what it's got to do with us.'

'She was stranded.'

'They'd have worked it out. He's probably still up there.'

'I can't believe she stays with him.'

'Jo-Jo, they've been together for ten years. If you ask me, they're as bad as each other.'

'You think that's a reasonable way for him to behave?'

'I'm just saying, she must know him by now.'

'Sulking. He's meant to be a man for God's sake.'


*Jo-Jo – July 2015*

---

I should have phoned him. Amy was right. Thirty-five years

89

after the event, and with Professor Hindsight on my shoulder, I could say with certainty I should have called him from the university. I should have fought harder to make it work, but back then the only thing that mattered was he'd promised to call me and he didn't. Anyway, I had the rest of my life to get on with and Amy didn't know the whole story. A week, two weeks, a month. Nothing. Thirty-five years and still nothing. He'd made a promise. My dad always said you should keep your promises. If he'd have phoned things might have been different, but how could I trust him if he couldn't even keep a promise?

I'd snapped at him again. This wasn't how the meal was meant to be. I wanted my sweet, innocent Freddie, making me laugh, looking up at me like I'd fallen from heaven to bless his life. I could sense he was still in there, lurking beneath this fractured ghost sitting opposite me.

'You never got the tooth done then?' I said.

He touched his mouth. 'No. Never had the money. Does it bother you?'

'I've always loved it, Freddie. You know that. It makes you unique.'

He smiled. 'Never seen another,' he said.

'Remind me how you did it.'

'Showing off to some girls. You know this story, Jo-Jo.'

'Do I?'

'I dived in the shallow end of the swimming pool and banged my head on the bottom. Why are you laughing?'

'It's just so un-Freddie like.'

'Yeah, well, I was eleven, learned my lesson at an early age. Never try to impress women.' He wiped his mouth with the napkin. 'I'm disappointing you aren't I?'

'No,' I said.

'Yes I am. I can see it in your face.'

'It's just…I didn't expect you to be so nervous. You never used to be.'

'That was a long time ago.'

'Maybe I should have left it where it belonged.'

'I'm still trying to work out why you didn't.'

'It felt like something I needed to do.'

He took a sip of water and looked around the conservatory, the older couple were having a break after their main course, the man had gone back to his paper; the woman was still searching for something in her handbag.

'It's a nice hotel,' said Freddie. 'Beats the curry Jack and I go for every month.'

'Perhaps we'd have been better in a nightclub.'

'Yeah,' he said 'I could have nailed the Pac-man record and you could have wowed them in your Go-Go boots.' He reached over and stroked the top of my hand with his right forefinger. 'I'm glad you decided to find me. Sorry I'm a bit of a wreck.'

'I wish you'd stop saying sorry,' I said.

\*\*\*

We walked side-by-side into the hotel reception. It was empty, apart from the nervy receptionist, who was obviously working the night shift. He was trying not to look at us, busying himself with moving pieces of paper around his desk. I wondered what he was thinking. Madam and her strange man, a secret liaison, the fiery daughter nowhere in sight. I'd have imagined a thousand scenarios at his age.

Freddie's nerves were back. He was probably wondering whether to kiss me or to shake my hand.

'Thank you for coming,' I said. 'It was nice.'

'I'm not going to say sorry again,' he said.

'No. Please don't.'

'When do you leave for New Zealand?' he said.

It was the first time either of us had mentioned my going away.

'I'm not sure. Amy's sorting it out.'

'Let me have your address,' he said. 'We can write, keep in touch.'

'I thought you weren't any good at writing.'

'Yeah, well. I've got better with age.'

It suddenly crossed my mind that Amy might be watching me. I scanned the reception area and into the conservatory. I'd told her to keep a low profile, but it wouldn't have surprised me if curiosity had driven her downstairs. I half expected to see her striding over the carpet, hand held out, announcing herself as the daughter. I had this image of Freddie and the receptionist bolting for the hills. I couldn't see her. Freddie was looking at me.

'I'd like to kiss you,' he said.

'I'd like that too.'

He leaned forward. I closed my eyes.

***

An hour later, I lowered myself into the white porcelain bath, held my nose, submerged and resurfaced. I wiped my eyes and rested the back of my head against the non-tap end, watching the steam rise towards the ceiling of the hotel bathroom, coconut smelling bubbles tickling my chin. The evening had ended okay. I wondered what he'd made of me. He'd remembered the boots, kept that memory with him all those years. He used to whimper slightly just before orgasming. What a thing to have in my head. The dance. I should have reminded him about our dance. Him trying so desperately to please me, to hold me properly, keeping his hands in the right places. He'd left before the hotel band had started. I'd imagined a dance, a last dance with my Freddie. At least he'd kissed me.

It started to rain as I pulled out of the hotel car park, turning into a full downpour as the journey progressed. I drove along the main road leading into the village, nearly back at my house, my eyes fixed on the shimmering tail lights of a Ford Focus. I concentrated hard. Thank God I hadn't had a drink. The fuzziness of the beta-blockers was bad enough. A lorry screamed past in the opposite direction, throwing up a splash of water, momentarily blocking out the world before the automatic wipers were triggered into a frenzy. A yellow haze from the street lights lit up a blurred bus stop queue, people standing in line, waiting patiently for the number 49; umbrellas drawn against the downpour. The brake lights from the Ford Focus lit up. 'Jesus,' I screamed, slamming my foot on the brake pedal, skidding the Mini to a stop. The engine stalled, honking horns sounded all around. I thumped the steering wheel. 'She must think I'm fucking mental,' I said.

*Freddie – September 1980*

I walked through the reception area of the Digbeth coach station and out into the empty main street. She'd gone. I stopped walking, looked up at the cloud filled sky and drew in a deep breath. It was always going to happen. She was always destined to do something else, be somewhere else. I told myself how lucky I'd been to have her in my life for a short, glorious time. I'd tried to keep her, begged her not to go, but it was inevitable. She wouldn't expect me to phone. She'd meet new friends, intelligent, interesting, good looking friends who could dance and knew how to use a knife and fork. Maybe it was time to let her go. I needed to talk to Jack.

*Freddie – December 1971*

---

I was playing Joseph in the nativity play; Elaine Clarke was playing the Angel Gabriel. I have a picture of us on stage, me sitting next to Sharon Barber, who played Mary, and kneeling in front of a wicker basket brought in by Miss Balsam, our math's teacher, to be used as a make-shift cradle. Elaine was standing behind us, wearing a full length white smock from the Art Department, polystyrene wings and a white tiara, holding a wand over our heads ready to bless the baby Jesus. I'm looking up at Elaine. Sharon's glancing sideways at me, a nervous smile on her face. My mum took the picture from the back of the packed hall, over the heads of the parents and teachers.

*Freddie – December 1981*

---

Max's. 2.30 A.M. The lights had come up and everyone was making their way to the exit. Elaine was slumped in a sofa, her wide eyes staring up at one of the mirror balls, a half empty glass of Bacardi and Coke in front of her. One of the waitresses was shaking her by the arm. 'Time to go now, love.'

I knelt down in front of the sofa. 'Elaine,' I said.

'She with you?' said the waitress.

'I know her from school,' I said.

'She's well gone. Been drinking that stuff all night. Blokes touching her up, getting a quick feel.'

'Elaine,' I said again, this time gently squeezing her arm.

She looked at me.

'It's Freddie,' I said. 'From school.'

'Freddie,' she said, touching my cheek. 'Where've you been, Freddie?'

'It's time to go home,' I said. 'The club's closing.'

'I want another drink,' she said, reaching out for the glass of Bacardi. 'Get me a drink, Freddie.'

The waitress grabbed her arm. 'No more drinks, love. It's time to go.'

'Get off me, you cow. Tell her, Freddie. Tell her to get off me.' She slumped back in the chair again.

'You taking her with you?' said the waitress.

'I can't. I don't know where she lives.'

'I don't think she cares which bed she's in. Could be your lucky night.'

*Freddie – July 2015*

I saw this film once about a manic robot. They were going to melt him down, but they operated instead. A lab technician unscrewed the top of his head. 'The circuitry's burnt out,' he said. 'We'll have to rewire him.' A second technician leaned forward. 'Disconnect the blue wire,' she said. 'That should do it. Calm him down a bit.' I wanted that operation. I wanted to reach inside my head and flick the switch to unclip my wires.

I pulled up outside Jack's house and blew out a deep breath, pleased to get his car back in one piece. I'd told him I'd post his keys through the letterbox, but I really wanted to tell him what had happened, talk it through with someone; not just be left with my own thoughts rattling around my head. I got out of the car and looked up at the house. The curtains were drawn, but his lounge light was on. I looked at my watch. Nine-thirty. I thought it was later. I wondered if Bob might be there. He had a key. Why hadn't Jack told me about the key? Perhaps staying the night was a regular thing. I walked up the driveway, went to ring the doorbell, stopped and pushed the keys through the letterbox. I walked back down the path, hands in my pockets and headed home.

***

2.00 A.M. I was sitting at my kitchen table, staring at the framed Jack Nicholson poster on my wall. I'd bought it off e-bay for ten pounds and then paid two hundred pounds to get it professionally framed. It was a cinema promotion for the film 'As Good As It Gets,' depicting a beaming Jack holding up Verdell, the Brussels Griffon dog, both looking lovingly into each other's faces.

I wondered what Jo-Jo was doing. I'd kissed her. One soft, gentle kiss. Not long. I was conscious of not lingering. That would have been inappropriate. It was our first kiss in over thirty years. She'd closed her eyes; I'd kept mine open. There was no clumsiness. Muscle memory. Our lips remembered how we fitted. That's what it felt like.

I replayed the meal over and over in my head. I remembered sweating and shaking a lot, but it seemed to finish okay. She was pleased I'd remembered the boots. She'd blushed when I'd mentioned them. The Jo-Jo I knew never blushed. That was always my job. Vegetarian. How could you go from adoring a blood steak to eating green salad and, hang on a minute, fish? I smiled. That sounded like a rule bender to me. I made a mental note to say that when I next saw her. We hadn't agreed a next time. She'd said she was going away. That's what the kiss was. A goodbye kiss.

I picked up the phone.

'What time is it?'

'I need to talk to you.'

'It's two in the morning.'

'I know. I was going to knock the door when I brought the car back, but I didn't want to disturb you.'

'So you thought you'd wait until two in the morning?'

'No. It's just… I've been thinking and… are you on your own?'

'What?'

'I thought Bob might be there.'

'We really need to sort out that head of yours, Freddie.'

'Can I come round?'

***

3.15 A.M. I was back in Jack's lounge. He'd laid out the coffee before I arrived and greeted me with a, 'this had better be good,' when he opened the front door. That put me on edge. I didn't really know what I was going to talk to him about. I told him about the meal, about the kiss. It all sounded a bit 'so what?' when I said it out loud.

There was a noise from the bedroom.

'It's the cat jumping off the bed, Freddie. He's wondering what everyone's doing awake in the middle of the night.'

'Sorry,' I said.

'What am I going to do with you?' he said, giving me a sad face look.

'I know. It's just, well, I needed to say it and you were the only one I could wake up at this hour.'

He laughed. 'I'm going to take that as a compliment.'

'Seriously, Jack, what should I do?'

'What do you want to do?'

'I don't know. She's leaving.'

'Maybe.'

'Her daughter's sorting everything out.'

He stood up, walked over to the lounge window and opened the curtains slightly to look out at the road. 'You'd better not have scratched the car,' he said.

'It's fine. You never told me how the wipers worked.'

'You can borrow it tomorrow if you want. I'm going to see Terry with Bob.' He turned and faced me. 'You need to tell her how you feel, Freddie.'

*****

2.30 P.M. the next day. I pulled into the hotel car park, this time parking the Mini in one of the visitor's spaces. The security guard was still standing by the bins, watching me with his arms folded. I wondered if he'd been home or if he lived at the hotel. He was looking at me as though I was casing the place for a robbery. I was half-tempted to give him the finger, but I decided against it.

I'd cat-napped on Jack's sofa, not able to face the anxiety of going back to my house, which meant I'd had to face it all in the morning when I went home to feed the cats. I'd phoned Jo-Jo from Jack's and said I wanted to see her, talk to her. She'd sounded surprised, asked what it was it was about, said yes, of course, come over to the hotel at three. I gave a vague answer to the 'what is it about' question, said I needed to ask her something, but I didn't want to do it over the phone. Ask her what? It was okay Jack saying tell her how you feel, nodding, smiling encouragement all the way through the call, but all I really knew was I didn't want her to go. I wanted to keep her in my life. Perhaps that's what I should say, see how she reacted. She'd have to let me down gently, say her family were waiting for her in New Zealand. I hadn't blown her away with my performance at the meal, but she had kissed me. Jack was right. I needed to try.

A woman walked out of the hotel exit, down the steps to the car park. She had bob cut auburn hair and was wearing a light tan leather bomber jacket, tight fitting black cord trousers and a pair of sunflower yellow pixie boots. She said something to the security guard who nodded, and then she walked with confident strides across the car park towards the visitor's spaces. I looked each side of me, trying to guess which car she was heading for.

She opened the passenger door of Jack's Mini.

'Are you Freddie?' she said.

'Yes, but how—'

She climbed into the passenger seat, shut the door, turned towards me and held out her hand. 'I'm Amy,' she said. 'I think you're here to see my mother.'

I stared at her nose freckles. She was still holding out her hand.

'Amy,' she repeated.

'I don't understand,' I said. 'I thought you lived in New Zealand.'

'I do. I've come to take Mum back with me. She told me you were coming, that she'd seen you last night. I've been waiting for you.'

I looked at the security guard.

'Mum doesn't know I'm here.'

'Right,' I said.

'I want to know what you're going to say to her. She said you'd phoned, that you had something to ask her.'

'That's between me and your mum,' I said.

'I don't want her upset. She's vulnerable.'

I looked at her. The daughter. The life without me. I couldn't imagine Jo-Jo vulnerable, but I did recognise this spit in your eye, bold as brass young woman as her daughter. 'You're so like your mum,' I said.

'What do you know about my mum?'

'Everything,' I said. 'And nothing. I probably don't know very much at all now, but I used to know everything.'

'Oh my God,' she said. 'You still love her.'

I looked out of the window. Neither of us said a word for a few minutes. I was listening to the birdsong from the surrounding wood, watching the still vigilant security guard. Amy suddenly reached out and gently flicked Mickey Mouse, making him bounce against the air vent.

'He's nice,' she said.

'I need to go,' I said, looking at the clock on the dashboard. 'I told your Mum I'd be there at three.'

'What are you going to say?'

'I really don't know.'

'You do love her though? Don't bother answering. I can tell. I don't understand how you can still love someone after thirty-five years of not seeing them.'

'That's because you're young,' I said.

'You're not mentally ill are you?'

I laughed. 'Maybe. What about you?'

'Mum said you have a daughter, but you don't see her.'

'That's none of your business.'

'I think it is if you're going to waltz into my life and take my mum away.'

'Take your mum away... Amy, we had dinner, most of which I spent sweating, stumbling over my words and trying to decide which fork to use. I'm here to say something I should have said years ago. I'll be lucky if your mum lets me finish the sentence before she sends me packing.'

'She won't send you packing.'

'Oh, I think she will. And she should. I've nothing to offer. I've never had anything to offer her.'

'She won't send you packing,' she said again.

This time I heard the certainty in her voice.

'Has your mum said something?'

'She doesn't need to say anything. When I ask about you she looks like you look when I ask about her. It's a bit nauseating actually.'

'No. You've got that wrong.'

'I thought you were going?' she said.

***

Amy left the car first, walked down the drive towards the main road, probably getting out of the way, not wanting to risk bumping into her mum in the reception area. I felt my heart rate increase, this time with excitement not anxiety, as it fought against the sedative effects of the beta-blockers. Maybe I wasn't such a lost cause. 'Carpe diem, Freddie,' Jack had said as I left his house. I told myself to calm down. Amy had said what she thought her mum was feeling. Nothing more. And even if Jo-Jo had feelings for me, it didn't mean she wanted me in her life. It was something though. That and the kiss. It was something.

## Jo-Jo – July 2015

After Freddie had gone, I realised I'd forgotten to ask him why he hadn't phoned all those years ago. Ancient history, history that should have been forgotten, but I still wanted to know the answer. And now he wanted to ask me something. I looked at my watch. He'd be here soon. Knowing Freddie and his obsession for organisation, he was probably here already. I went over to the window in the reception area, my eyes scanning the car park for Jack's Mini. I spotted the car. The passenger door opened and Amy got out. She walked down the driveway. I could see Freddie still sitting in the driver's seat.

I walked, half ran, outside and headed towards the car.

Freddie was walking towards me. 'Jo-Jo,' he said.

'Was that Amy in your car?' I said.

He looked back down the drive. 'She wanted to vet me I think before we met up again.'

'How did she know you?'

He nodded towards the security guard. 'I think Clouseau

helped. He saw me last night. Did you tell her we were meeting today?'

'Damn cheek,' I said, looking at the security guard. 'I've a good mind to report him.'

'I don't think he meant any harm.'

'I'm cross with Amy too.'

'She asked me what my intentions were.'

I laughed. 'Your intentions? I don't think my dad ever asked you that question.'

'Thank God for that,' he said. 'Perhaps he should have. It might have woken me up a bit.' He held out his hand. 'Shall we go for a walk?'

Something had happened to him since last night. I held his arm and we walked across to the hotel gardens. We sat down on one of the benches underneath a eucalyptus tree, the smell reminding me of the olbas oil Dad used to put on our pillows if we had blocked noses and couldn't sleep.

'She's a romantic your daughter.'

'She can get carried away,' I said.

'She reminds me of you.'

'Amy? She's nothing like me.'

'She's got your nose freckles.'

I reached up and touched my nose. I wondered where this was heading, what he was going to say next. I felt a roll of anxiety in my stomach. What had Amy said to him?

'Do you remember when we met?' he said. 'That dance. I always wondered why you asked me.'

'It's a good job I did. I'd still be waiting for you to ask me.'

'You were way out of my league, Jo-Jo.'

'You should believe in yourself more.'

'You sound like Jack.'

'And that makes Jack and me right.'

'I've missed you, Jo-Jo. All those years. I've never stopped thinking about you.'

'We were kids, Freddie. Things at that age matter more, stay with you longer.'

'I don't want you to go,' he said, blurting it out as though it was something he'd had wedged in his throat for decades. 'I don't want to lose you again.'

And there it was. We were back in my room, on my bed, lying underneath my Starsky and Hutch poster, Freddie asking me not to go, me not giving in, resisting his sulks, his emotional blackmail. I had ambition, hope and the rest of my life in front of me. I wanted to do something, nothing was going to get in my way. Nothing. He promised to phone. He was meant to phone.

*Jo-Jo – December 1980*

---

Patrick Donovan it said on the name badge hanging from the interior mirror of the black cab. 'You're my last fare,' he said. 'Be glad to get home and put me feet up. I've got a bottle of Murphy's cooling in the fridge.' I told him the name of the road. 'Moor Park. I'll tell you where to stop.'

'I'm not a miracle worker, love. I need to know the address.'

'I'll show you when we get there.' He told me about his family, his teenage daughters, what a handful they were. 'I bet you're the same. Giving your dad the run-around, driving him crazy.' I didn't answer. He stopped talking.

Twenty minutes later, he turned the taxi into a tree lined avenue of 1950's council houses. 'Here we are, love, Moor Park. Worth a fortune these. Where do you want me to stop?'

'Just here on the right.'

'What's this place then?'

He peered through the windscreen and read aloud the name inscribed on the stilt mounted wooden sign at the front of the building: 'Faith Hill Clinic'. I watched him as he read, waiting for the realisation to dawn. His face crumpled. I could sense he was cursing himself for not realising. All that talk about his family, his children. He turned and faced me. 'You okay, love?' he said. 'Are you on your own?'

'I'm fine. How much do I owe you?'

'Sixteen-eighty,' he said.

I handed him a twenty pound note. 'Keep the change,' I said.

'You look after yourself, love.'

I climbed out of the taxi, clutching my mum's carpet bag, and walked up the gravel driveway. I took a deep breath and told myself again it was the right decision. I had the rest of my life to think about. I could feel the taxi driver watching me. I imagined him trying to guess my age, comparing me with his kids, hoping and praying they would never have to go anywhere near a place like this, not now, not ever. Maybe he would give them an extra hug when he got home.

*** 

A smiling receptionist, heavily made up face, bright red lipstick, hair tied up in in a bun. She wanted to know my name. Waiting room. Cold blue plastic seats, contraception posters, coffee table magazines, Women's Own, Woman's Weekly, Women's Realm. Three other women. No-one speaking, no-one reading. Everyone staring straight ahead. Pale faces. Scared eyes. Form filling. Questions. Father's name. Unknown. Dry mouth. A sip of water.

More waiting.

The gown, the bed, the paper sheet. The doctor, the only man, looking down at me, softly spoken, welsh accent, thin rimmed spectacles precariously perched on the edge of his nose. Poke, prod, scratch, counting down from ten – nine, eight, seven.

Darkness.

I could hear someone crying.

Wake-up.

Pain. Painkillers. A cup of sweet tea.

Leaflets. Counselling. Contraception.

Another taxi. Street lights. Stale tobacco smell. Traffic noise.
Throwing up.

More crying.


*Jo-Jo – A Memory*

---

I'm six. Dad's bought a bright red swing from Woolworths and set it up in the centre of his newly laid lawn. I watch as Josh pokes a bamboo cane into the rhubarb patch, trying to annoy the wasps.

'All done,' shouts Dad. 'Who wants first go?'

'Me,' I shout, running over to the swing and jumping on the seat.

'That's not fair,' says Josh, throwing his stick up the garden. 'You're too old for swings.'

'You'll both get a turn,' says Dad. 'Now, hold on tight, young lady.'

He pushes me gently at first and then with more and more force.

'Higher,' I shout, the wind rushing against my face. 'I want to go higher.' I close my eyes and squeal louder and louder. 'Higher. Higher. Higher.'

Dad runs to the front of the swing. He claps his hands and holds out his arms. 'Jump,' he says as I head skywards.

'I can't. I can't.'

He claps his hands again. 'Jump, my darling. Jump. I'll catch you. I promise I'll catch you.'

I shake my head and laugh as the swing goes back up.

'Jump,' he says again as the swing heads back towards him.

I let go. Two seconds flying through the air. He catches me, squeezes me close and slides me slowly to the floor. He kisses my forehead. 'Well done,' he says. 'My big, brave girl.'

'That was great, Dad. Can we do again?'

'Of course we can, sweetheart.'

'My turn,' says Josh.

'Okay,' says Dad, ruffling Josh's hair. 'Let me check on your mum first.'

I look at Josh, who is looking at the floor.

'Come on,' I say. 'I'll push you until Dad gets back.'


*Freddie – November 1980*

---

7.30 A.M. We ran along platform two at Walsall railway station, drizzling rain and fog soaking into my bones. I'd forgotten my gloves and I could feel the ends of my fingers going numb.

We jumped onto the train. A whistle sounded and we hurried along the corridor, looking for an empty carriage.

'Here's one,' said Jack, dragging me inside.

Our black Adidas sports bags landed with a thud in the overhead luggage shelf and we dropped into the blue velour covered seats, Jack sitting down diagonally opposite me and putting his feet up on the vacant seat at my side. I put my feet up on the seat next to him and flopped my head back, staring up at the white plastic ceiling. The train moved slowly out of the station.

'That was close,' he said. 'How come you were late?'

'I had to sort Mum's breakfast. You know what she's like. '

'Is she okay?'

'She'll be fine.'

'I'll go round if you want to stay.'

I closed my eyes.

De-dum… de-dum … de-dum… de-dum.

The speed of the train increased.

De-dum, de-dum, de-dum, de-dum.

I felt Jack pat my leg and I opened my eyes. He was leaning forward in his seat. I sat up, dropping my legs to the floor. 'I was awake all night,' I said.

'I told you to phone.'

'I want it to be a surprise.'

'It'll be that all right. She's been up there a month and you've not even called.'

'I know. I needed to sort my head out.'

He smiled and patted my leg again. 'It'll be fine. Tell her it was the shock of her leaving.'

'I will. As soon as I see her.'

'You've got the address?'

I patted the pocket of my denim jacket. 'Thanks for coming with me, Jack. I need the moral support.'

'No problem. That's my job. What else was I going to do on a wet November day?'

A train sped past in the opposite direction.

'What's the plan when we get there?'

I shrugged. 'Jump in a taxi I suppose.'

He put his feet back up on the chair. 'I hope she's there,' he said. 'I'll wait for you at the station, grab a coffee or something. If you're not back in an hour I'm coming home.'

\*\*\*

We walked into the greasy spoon opposite Lincoln station. It felt like we'd undulated our way across every inch of every one-horse town on route.

Jack ordered a full English and a mug of tea. 'Extra black

pudding,' he said to the pot-bellied lank-haired man behind the counter. 'And he's paying.'

The tables were covered in fruit patterned wipe-easy plastic tablecloths. We sat down at one near the window. Jack picked up the plastic tomato and squished red sauce all over his breakfast.

'You know they never clean those,' I said. 'God knows what's living in the spout.'

'You worry too much. Are you not having anything to eat?'

'I can't. I need to get this over with.'

I left him to his double fried eggs, sausage, bacon, fried bread and extra black pudding and walked across the road to the taxi rank, climbing into the back of the first black cab.

'Dimbles Lane,' I said.

'Long road that, mate. You got a number?'

'Eighteen. How far is it?'

'Ten minutes.'

I settled back in the seat. The driver pulled his interior window across, not interested in any more chat, which I welcomed. I needed to get my head straight, think through what I was going to say. I asked myself again why I'd made it so complicated. We'd sorted it out. She'd sorted it out. I'd go up the following weekend and help her settle in. That's what we'd agreed. But I was never going to go. I'd closed her down in my head. She needed to move on. We'd done our time. It was Jack who changed my mind.

'Where are you going to meet someone else like her, Freddie?'

'That's the point. I'm punching above my weight. She'll realise that sooner or later.'

'Only one problem with that theory, dick-head. She seems to want you to stick around. God knows why. I'd have dropped you after that first dance.'

It took me two weeks of pondering, lying in bed for most of the day, thinking it through. Jack was right. Blackpool. Max's.

Chatting. Laughing. Kissing. Making Love. We fitted. But she'd still left me. Had she? 'I have to do this, Freddie.' 'It's only Lincoln.' 'Come and help me settle in.'

'Okay. I'll go and see her, but I want it to be a surprise.'

'Why?'

'I just do. I want to see how she reacts.'

'Jesus, Freddie. You can be such hard work.'

'Will you come with me?'

'I'm not talking to her for you. You can sort that yourself.'

The taxi came to a stop.

'Dimbles Lane, mate,' said the driver. 'I think number eighteen's in there.'

I looked out of the window at the only block of three-storey flats. It was completely out of place in the long row of 1950's steel framed houses, which were all painted buttercup yellow. It started to rain.

'Three-fifty,' said the driver, clearly anxious to get on with his next fare.

I reached into the pocket of my jeans, mentally keeping a tab on how much this trip had cost me so far – Jack's train fare, his breakfast, the taxi. The front door of the flats swung open and I heard Jo-Jo laugh.

She stepped out through the open door and opened up a pink umbrella. It was only spotting with rain, but she wouldn't have wanted to get her hair wet. A man walked out behind her, wearing a bowler hat, a full-length Crombie coat and red Doc Martens. He said something to Jo-Jo. She tapped him playfully on the back and then carried on wrestling the umbrella open. The man offered his arm, which Jo-Jo accepted and they turned right, walking away from the cab; arm in arm, chatting, laughing.

'You okay, mate?'

'Yeah. I'm fine. I've changed my mind. Can you take me back to the station?'

'What's with the hat?'

Shelley man shrugged. 'It's a look,' he said, lifting up his right foot and tapping his red Doc Marten. 'And it goes with the boots.'

I laughed.

'Liam,' he said, holding out his hand.

'Jo-Jo,' I said.

'So, Jo-Jo, tell me what brings you on this coach.'

Liam. My university best friend, protector, counsellor and mentor. Sixteen years older than me, he used to work nights as a mortuary attendant, sitting with the dead, collecting them from the wards, helping put their organs back in the body, sewing up the carcass after the post mortem. One night, his radio came on all by itself. 'Three o'clock in the morning,' he said. 'I decided it was time to get out.' We sat next to each other in seminars and lectures, spent our time chatting about nothing and everything in the local pub over pints of Mackeson and Vimto, swopped books by Chekhov and Turgenev, which we read drinking vodka shots into the early hours of the morning, wallowing away long weekends in the company of Princesses, duelling Counts and innocent first love. We once spent a rainy Sunday reading Edith Wharton's 'Ethan Frome', him finishing first, lying on a battered leather sofa, pulling his bowler hat over his eyes and grinning at me as I worked my way through the last few chapters. 'Don't tell me,' I said, racing to the conclusion. 'I wouldn't dare,' he said, lifting up his hat and watching me closely, joy smothering his face as I gasped at the tragic ending.

I told him all about Freddie five minutes into the coach journey.

'You'll meet him next week,' I said. 'He's coming to visit.'

'Shame he couldn't help you settle in though.'

'Yes,' I said, looking out of the window.

8.00 P.M. My second taxi of the day pulled up outside the block of flats, a mile from the university. Liam had rented a two bedroom flat rather than stay on campus and had asked me to share with him. 'I can't. I don't even know you.' That wasn't true. I had known him for two months before he'd asked the question and by that time it was obvious Freddie had made his choice, and I had to make mine. 'I'm not interested in a relationship, Liam.'

'Don't flatter yourself,' he said. 'I just need someone to share the rent.'

I pushed open the rear door of the black cab and vomited into the gutter.

'Shall I get someone?' said the driver, not moving out of his seat.

'How much?' I spluttered.

'What?'

'The fare. How much do I owe you?'

I thrust a twenty pound note into his hand, grabbed my carpet bag, which I'd clutched tight the whole journey, and looked up at the second floor of the flats. The after effects of the anaesthetic were blurring my vision, but, through the haze of the December evening, I could see there were no lights on. Good. Liam was out. I tried to stand, but my right foot slid on the greasy pavement. I grabbed the door to steady myself. I heard the driver sigh. He'd obviously looked at me, my age and decided I was drunk. I should have stayed overnight, they'd insisted I stay, but I'd told them I'd be fine. Yes, there was someone at home to look after me. Three hours they'd made me wait. I'd have sprinted out of the operating theatre door to get away, leave it all behind. I tried to stand again. The painkillers were wearing off. If I could only get up to the flat, get into bed.

'Jo-Jo.'

Liam ran up to the cab. 'What's wrong?' he said, grabbing my arm.

I dropped back down on the seat. 'I'm okay. Just get me in the flat.'

He grabbed my bag, threw it over his shoulder. 'Come on,' he said, putting his arm around my waist and helping me to my feet. He looked inside the cab at the driver. 'Prick,' he said.

'Nothing to do with me, mate. She should learn to hold her drink.'

'Please,' I said. 'Just get me inside.'

## Jo-Jo's Dream

I throw the knife onto the draining board, drips of blood splash into the potato water.

'Are you okay?'

'I'm fine.'

'Let me see.'

'It's nothing,' I say, sucking the end of my finger.

'I want to meet him.'

'That's never going to happen.'

'How long?'

'Jason, please, I've told you everything.'

'How long were you seeing him?'

Silence.

'We'll go today.'

'It's over. I'm not going.'

I'm in the Mazda, outside the house, rain bouncing off the car roof. I turn towards the passenger seat.

'I was coming back to you. Why don't you believe me?'

'Was he better than me?'

Silence.

'I said—'

'—I heard you.'

'Then why aren't you answering me?'

'Please can we go home?'

'I want to see him.'

'You know I love you.'

'I need to see him.'

'Why are you making me do this?'

'You know why.'

Silence.

I open the car door, step out into the storm, pull the hoodless anorak tight and crunch up the gravel path. The security light responds to my presence. I reach the front door and hesitate.

'Ring it. Ring it now.'

I press the bell, rain dripping off my face.

The house stays in darkness.

I press the bell again.

The hallway light comes on. My stomach drops. The door opens.

'Good God, Jo-Jo, you're soaked—'

'—It's Jason,' I say.

'Jason?'

'He's here, Freddie.'

'Come inside, sweetheart. You'll catch your death.'

'You mustn't touch me. He's watching. Tell him. Please tell him.'

He pulls me close, kisses the top of my head. 'Jason's dead, sweetheart.'

I push him away. 'Don't say that. You must tell him.'

'I don't understand.'

'That I was going back to him. The night he died. The car crash.'

He hugs me, no resistance this time. 'You were never going back, my darling. It was over. Let's get you some dry clothes.'

'No,' I say, looking back at the empty car. 'That's not true. I was coming home to you.'

## Jo-Jo – December 1980

I was sitting on the bed waiting for Liam to come back.

'Here,' he said, rushing into the room, a glass of water in one hand and a washing up bowl in the other.

I took the glass, unzipped the side pocket of my carpet bag and fetched out a foil sachet. I popped two of the Tramadol tablets clear of the foil, put them in my mouth, took a sip of water and swallowed. Liam was watching me. He was still holding the bowl.

'I don't think I need that now.'

He put it on the floor next to the bed. 'Just in case,' he said, sitting down next to me and taking my hand.

'You going to tell me what's going on?'

'Not now. I need to sleep.'

'I only went out for a bottle of wine.'

'I'll stick with the morphine if that's okay with you.'

He looked at the sachet. 'Jo-Jo,' he said.

'I'm fine, Liam. I just need to rest.'

His kindness over the days and weeks following my visit to that place cemented the foundation for our friendship. I worried about him being Irish, waited for some sermon on the rights and wrongs, but if he thought it, he didn't let it show. He served me breakfast in bed, two boiled eggs with bread and butter soldiers and a pot of tea.

'I'll get us a chicken for tonight,' he said. 'Mother always swore by a roast dinner to get you back on your feet.'

'I'm not six, Liam.'

'Course you're not,' he said, patting my leg. 'What vegetables do you want?'

Liam and I had arranged to meet at the Three Chimneys pub, which was up the hill on the edge of the market, away from the centre of town and the regular student haunts. I was a bit early and, rather than walk inside on my own, I waited for him in a shop doorway. It was Mum's fault, always let the man lead she'd say, which was okay for her because she had Dad.

Liam appeared, swaggering his way through the empty square, his Crombie coat smacking against his legs, his closed umbrella held aloft in salute.

I looked around the empty stalls.

Two workmen, who had been sweeping up the discarded fish and chip wrappings, pizza boxes and crunched up Coca-Cola tins, were now leaning on their brooms and staring; further along the pavement a man and woman out walking their Jack Russell dog shook their heads and whispered something to each other.

Liam reached me. We hugged. 'Why didn't you wait inside?' he said.

I shrugged.

'It's not because you're a girl, surely?'

No,' I said, hitting him on the arm.

He pushed the door and held it open, gesturing for me to walk across the threshold. 'Then lead the way. The first round's on you.'

I walked over the sticky blue carpet towards the bar, feeling every lift of my trainers as they sucked away from the nylon fibre. 10cc's 'Dreadlock Holiday' was playing on the jukebox, Liam was walking two paces behind me. I sat down on one of the worn leather stools and looked around, wondering why I'd chosen this sink pit of a pub. The place was empty apart from a man leaning against the far wall. He was picking at his finger nails, greasy hair matted to his scalp, a food-stained Led Zeppelin t-shirt not quite covering his stomach paunch. My eyes fell on the line of black pubic hair poking out through the top of his track suit bottoms. I quickly looked away.

A smiling barmaid walked out from the back room. 'What can I get you?' she said, furrowing her brow and glaring at Liam.

I ordered a pint of lager and blackcurrant.

'Ah, my friend chooses a fine beverage,' said Liam, standing at my side. 'I'll have the same.'

The barmaid pulled the pints, all the time giving Liam a hard stare.

'Is he always like that?' she said

I nodded, which prompted Liam to reach into his wallet and, as though he were a magician revealing shiny items from a top hat, he theatrically pulled out two, one pound notes and waved them in the barmaid's face. 'Keep the change,' he said, winking at her.

She took the money without a word and disappeared into the sanctuary of her snug.

'She thinks you're mad,' I said.

'Good,' he said. 'How tedious to be thought of as sane. Shall we move to a table?'

I took a sip of beer and we walked over to a small round table by the window. I could see the workmen still sweeping the streets. We sat down. The table rocked. I tore a beer mat in half and placed it under one of the legs. I could feel Liam watching me. He kept touching the top of his nose stud.

'You okay,' he said.

'No,' I said. 'I miss him.'


*Jo-Jo – April 1981*

---

I went to a house-party being thrown by someone in Liam's poetry circle, the first time I'd braved the world after the clinic.

'It'll do you good,' said Liam.

After about half-an-hour of smiling and pretending to socialise, I noticed a man about Liam's age sitting in a leather Sherlock chair, reading the Guardian. He wore a tweed suit and had hooded eyelids that reminded me of an eagle I'd seen at the zoo on a day trip with Dad. Chaos reigned all around, Madness' 'Night Train to Cairo' was blasting out of the stereo, congoing students with glasses of Bacardi and coke in hand. One of the lads flicked the newspaper and shouted, 'Come on, Professor. Let's see what you've got.'

'Who's that?' I said to Liam.

'Prof Jolly. He's one of the seminar tutors. He's a bit of an oddball.'

'Says the man in the bowler hat.'

'Touché,' he said, giving a full length bow.

'He looks sad.'

'Sad? Not really thought about it.'

I looked around the room. 'Who's he here with?'

'No-one,' said Liam, smiling. 'You really are a sucker for lost causes.'

'Shoot me. I like to see everyone happy. That's not a crime is it?'

'No. It's sweet. Shall I introduce you?'

*Jo-Jo – May 1981*

---

Back at the flat, two weeks after Dad's funeral, Liam had cooked us ribeye steaks with mushroom sauce. Dirty pots and pans filled every work surface, which they always did when Liam cooked. His pièce de résistance was Tiramisu, which he only ever made as a treat for me. 'It's not right, Jo-Jo. The coffee ruins a good trifle.'

We moved into the lounge, away from the dirty crocks – out of sight, out of mind – me carrying a bottle of Merlot, our second of the night. I'd already filled both our glasses. He stretched out on the cracked brown leather sofa and I dropped into the chair, draping my legs over the arm.

'You never talk about your family, Liam.'

He took a sip of wine. 'This is nice,' he said. 'Did you buy it from the supermarket?'

I shook my head. 'The shop on the estate. He's getting used to us now. Said he doesn't mind stocking it as long as it sells. You changed the subject.'

'It's complicated,' he said.

I'd tried a couple of times to have this conversation, to find out why a man in his mid-thirties had no past, like a time-traveller from the future with no history in the present. I'd put his lack of interest in me down to our age difference, but there were plenty of women his age who'd have been interested and he never responded.

'You always say that.'

'Let it go, Jo-Jo. It's private.'

'I thought we were friends.'

'We are... let's change the subject.'

'It's okay if you're gay.'

'Gay?'

'Yes. It's no big deal these days. It doesn't bother me.'

'I'm not gay, Jo-Jo.'

'Okay. I'm just saying if you were, it wouldn't be a problem.'

He sat up and put his wine glass down on the coffee table. 'You're not going to give up on this are you?'

'I'd like to know who I'm living with and, if we're friends, you should trust me. I tell you everything.'

He stood up and walked over to the door. 'It's not about trust,' he snapped.

His face creased up and he burst into tears.

I jumped up out of the chair, rushed over to him and hugged him. 'Oh God, Liam. Ignore me. I'm just drunk and feeling sad about Dad… and I'm a nosy cow.'

He kissed the top of my head.

I looked up at him. He was wiping his eyes.

'You are a nosy cow,' he said.

'Let's forget I mentioned it. Go back to our wine. I'll never ask again.'

He shook his head. 'No. You're right. We're friends and we live together.'

'So what. Private is private. I don't want you upset.'

'I should talk about it, Jo-Jo, but I don't think you'll like me very much after I've told you.'

I stepped back. 'What do you mean?' I said.

He walked back to the sofa, took a gulp of wine and held out his glass. I fetched the Merlot from the side of the chair and filled the glass half way.

He shook it at me. 'Fill it up,' he said 'I'm going to need it.'

I did as he asked. His hands were shaking. The blood had drained from his face.

I sat back down, filled up my glass and looked at him expectantly. 'You're frightening me, Liam. What is it?'

'I'm not exactly the good guy in this story, Jo-Jo. So just let me tell it. No questions. And then we'll see how you feel about me.'

'Okay,' I said. 'If you're sure you want to tell me.'

He took another slurp of wine, put his glass down, leaned forward, gripping his hands in a prayer like pose, the ends of his fingers anaemic, the blood draining away from the tips as he told his story to the carpet.

Married, Jenny, childhood sweethearts, little girl, Rosie, five years of age. And then he met her. The other woman. The cliché. I gulped down a mouthful of Merlot, fought the urge to stay in my seat. He looked up at me.

'I know what you're thinking.'

'I'm not thinking anything. I'm listening.'

The lie was obvious. I tried to push away the disapproving look I could feel on my face, tried to smile reassuringly, but it was forced, hard. He looked at the carpet again. I had to say something.

'Who was she?'

'No-one.'

'I don't understand.'

'It doesn't matter who she was.'

'You're not making sense, Liam. If she broke up your marriage—'

'—My wife and daughter are dead.'

He said the sentence as though he was on speed, the words falling out of his mouth in a lump, a tumour.

'Dead? My God. What happened?'

'I killed them,' he said.

My stomach dropped. It flashed across my mind that I didn't really know him. He was still leaning forward, hands clasped, staring at the floor. I looked towards the lounge door. It was behind the sofa, behind Liam. I looked at him. He was staring at me through tear-filled eyes. His whole face had crumpled in on itself.

'I don't mean literally, but I might as well have done.'

I stood up, walked over to the sofa, sat down and put my arm around him.

'Just tell me what happened.'

He looked at the carpet again.

'I was with her. Some run-down hotel that let you book rooms by the day. We'd used it a couple of times before. Jenny followed me. I thought we'd been careful.'

'Your wife came to the hotel?'

'Came up to the room. I opened the door in a dressing gown. She had Rosie in her arms. Never said a word. Looked at me, looked at the crumpled double bed and just walked off down the corridor.'

'What did you do?'

'I went after her, but she was like a zombie, staring straight through me. Rosie was crying. Everyone was staring at us in the reception area. I asked her to wait while I got dressed, but she strapped Rosie in her seat, got in her car and drove off.'

He stopped talking. I hugged him closer, waiting for him to carry on, dreading what was coming next.

'I never saw them again,' he said. 'Not alive.'

He finished the story quickly, taking big gulps of air to help him through. Jenny's car ploughed into a combine harvester about a mile away from the hotel. She'd just overtaken a cyclist along a narrow country lane. The cyclist escaped with minor injuries, the driver of the combine harvester was treated for shock, Jenny and Rosie died instantaneously.

'She never drove like that. It was me. I killed them.'

I hugged him to me. I couldn't think of anything to say.


*Jo-Jo's Dream*

---

A prism of white light falls into the bedroom, hanging from the ceiling like a stalactite about four feet away from me. Something moves inside the frosty veneer.

'What is that?'

'It's your audience.'

I stare hard. Dad's woman stares back through the white light, but it's a three foot high puppet version secured to the sides of the prism, strings attached to each of her limbs, pulling her arms and legs up and down in a slow dance, a ghostly waltz.

I reach out a hand.

'She can't hear or see you.'

'But what's she doing here?'

'She needs your forgiveness to set her free.'

'She'll be dancing a long time before I forgive her.'

*Freddie – August 1981*

---

I bumped into Alison in the Telford shopping centre. I saw her walking out of Boots as I was heading towards HMV. I dropped my eyes, but it was too late. 'Freddie,' she shouted. I smiled and she came over. I looked behind her, expecting to see Ted.

'Hi,' I said. 'Fancy seeing you here.'

'I'm with my mum,' she said. 'This is the only town round here with a Debenhams. Where's Jo-Jo?'

'University. She's in Lincoln.'

'That must be hard.'

'We split up. I miss her.'

'You must,' she said, touching my arm and dropping her bottom lip. 'You seemed so close.'

I realised it was the first time I'd said I missed Jo-Jo out loud. I'd refused to talk to Jack about it since we'd come back from Lincoln and had spent most of the year staring at the artex swirls on my bedroom ceiling, thinking about what she might be doing, the guy I'd seen her with, trying to convince myself it was no big deal, people split up all the time. All I needed to do was move on with my life. But I hadn't. I'd stayed with her in my head, spooling the memories over and over and over, and now it was all on the verge of pouring out...to Aran wool cardigan Alison... here in the town centre.

'Where's Ted?' I said, trying desperately to change the subject.

'We split up as well,' she said.

Alison and I saw each other for about two months, me

talking about Jo-Jo, her telling me about Ted. It felt like a healing, cathartic process for us both, interrupted by occasional bouts of tension relieving sex. When we'd finished talking about loss, when the grieving had come to an end, the relationship fizzled out like flat pop. She stopped calling. I stopped calling. The next thing I knew six months had gone by and we hadn't spoken. Alison got me away from the artex, and I went back to Max's with Jack.

*Freddie – May 1985*

---

I started working nights in one of the local care homes. One of the staff had left to have a baby and I got the job. 'It'll be good to have a man,' said Matron. 'Someone to change the light bulbs.'

Most of the care staff were middle-aged women, but I was paired with Lorraine because she was closer to my age, only ten years older than me. She had tightly cropped, bleached blonde hair and olive skin, which I found out later was a gene present from a Maltese great-grandfather. Her red dress uniform fascinated me from the start, with its purple press studs running down its full length. She wore it just above her knee, leaving the last two studs unfastened. One night, about two in the morning, the home was graveyard quiet and we made a cup of coffee, pulled a couple of lounge chairs together and sat with our feet up, listening out for any call bells or Matron sneaking up from the sleeping-in room to try and catch us asleep. Lorraine caught me staring at her legs. 'You see anything you want?' she said. I lowered my eyes, my cheeks on fire. She stood up and turned my head back towards her. 'Ask me?'

'Ask you what?' I said. She reached out and guided my hands to the hem of her uniform. 'Open it,' she said. I hesitated. 'Go on,' she said. I gently pulled and two of the studs popped open. I could see the top of her stockings and the start of bare flesh. 'Open the rest, Freddie,' she said.

We had sex every night we worked a shift together, usually in one of the empty rooms, lying down on the unmade bed in the cocoon of the home, neither of us saying a word, her dress open, my shirt unfastened, our bare flesh making forbidden contact. Her cold marriage made her cry. 'He's a pig and he's not shy of giving me a back-hander.' I kissed her tears, told her over and over I'd look after her, it would all be okay. I had no idea what that meant, but it seemed like the right thing to say. The Commodores 'Night Shift' became our song. We never saw each other outside of work.

And then she told me she was pregnant.

'It can't be his. He never touches me.'

*Freddie's Book*

---

Night had fallen. There was a full moon reflecting off a rippling lake, showing up legions of pond hoppers skating across fresh green lily palms and a swarm of mosquitoes hovering at the water's edge. A blanket of mist suddenly dropped, shrouding the neighbour's conifers in ribbons of fog, which were chasing each other like a posse of ghosts in an elaborate game of twister. A whisper of wind lifted the mist slightly and, Chardonnay gasped, sitting in the middle of the lake were a row of four smoke humans. They broke into a smile, as though someone had flicked on a power switch, and started to make a deep pitched, baritone hum.

Chardonnay turned to Luther.

'Lost souls,' he said. 'Lost souls waiting for a new life.'

She looked back at the ghosts. Eyes, nose, mouth, everything human was there, but it was fading in and out of existence, struggling to anchor a grip in time and space. The humming slowly increased its volume, working its way through the vocal ranges. It hit soprano level and the ghosts threw their hands skywards, their black eyes staring expectantly towards the heavens.

'What are they doing?'

'Calling to God, young lady. They're trying to attract his attention.'

'Does he ever hear them?'

'Maybe one day he will.'

The hum stepped up another pitch, and then another, louder and louder.

*Freddie – October 1985*

---

Lorraine. The Lost City girl. She'd learned to swim in the canal, had cousins who were roaming gypsies, and she could ride a horse bare back by the time she was ten. Everyone owned a horse. They were tethered on every spare patch of grass. People rode them to the White Swan, the estate pub, and tied them to the wooden pole outside; pony and trap races were common place down the main street, crowds gathering to place their bets.

She told her husband, Keith, about us and, fuelled by Johnny Walker, he walked up to the home in the middle of the night and back-heeled his Doc Martens into each of the door panels of my Ford Fiesta. It had taken me months of working overtime to save for that car. The police arrested him, kept him in a cell overnight. 'You're welcome to her,' he shouted at me as I arrived for work one evening.

'He doesn't love me,' said Lorraine. 'I think the pregnancy's upset him.'

Keith told everyone. 'God knows who was looking after the

residents while they were at it,' he said. Matron called us into the office. 'I need to put you on different rotas.' We knew that wouldn't work. She didn't have that many staff. Lorraine shrugged. 'I'll have the kid soon. I can't work then anyway.' I hadn't thought about that.

We found a maisonette for rent and moved in together. Lorraine cooked us a full English breakfast, including black pudding and bubble and squeak, which we covered in brown sauce and ate in bed. We slept until the middle of the afternoon, took a bath together and went back to bed until tea-time. I fetched a Chinese take-away and we watched Miami Vice on a black and white portable television I'd brought with me from my mum's. We went to work at ten o'clock. Affair, pregnancy, living together, sleeping with each other every day, working side-by-side at night. Five months in, the pregnancy started to show, the morning sickness kicked in and Lorraine went off on maternity leave.

'You're going be a great dad, Freddie.'

Dad. I was seven years old when he left me. I knew what a mum was, but I had no idea about being a dad.


*Freddie – A Memory*

---

We're in the delivery room. Lorraine is two weeks overdue and the hospital staff have made the decision to break her waters. 'No epidural, Freddie. I want it to be natural. That's what we deserve.' I nod sagely as though I understand every word. I'm fully gowned up, a paper mask covering my mouth. Lorraine is squeezing my hand tighter and tighter with every contraction. She screams at the nurse for something to take away the pain. The nurse nods and fetches the doctor. Two hours go by and the top of Becky's head enters the world. 'Would Dad like to see?' All eyes face me, everyone's waiting for me to react. Black matted hair, blood and mucous is what I see. I look back at Lorraine. 'It's a baby,' I say, trying to sound proud, emotional. The nurse grins. 'Thank God for that,' she says. 'Get ready to cut the cord, Dad.'


*Freddie's Book*

---

From the side of the glass atrium, identical twins with red witch hair, milky translucent skin and wide, all knowing owl eyes, pulled a tarpaulin covered wooden hand cart into view. The twins were wearing cat suits made out of sickle-shaped veiny leaves, tightly woven together by strands of different coloured grasses. The veins pulsed with life.

God stroked the hair of each twin in greeting and turned back to the crowd.

'Shall we see what's in the cart?'

'Soul mates; Soul mates; Soul mates'

'I can't hear you. What did you say?'

'Soul mates; Soul mates; Soul mates'

God lifted a corner of the tarpaulin. The crowd fell silent.

'Patience, my people. The soul-mates will be revealed, but we need to return to the arbitration.

All eyes fell back on Chardonnay.


*Freddie – February 1986*

---

We'd all gathered for visiting time on the second floor maternity ward at New Cross hospital. Lorraine's bed, the last in a row, overlooked a wood and there was lots of bird song drifting in through the draughty full length window.

I looked around the bed at my ready-made in-laws.

Doreen. The Mum. Black framed NHS bifocal spectacles perched on the end of her nose, receding ginger hair parted in the centre, thick black tights, laughing at her own jokes, worshipping Black Country food, grey peas, faggots, jellied eels, pig's tails and trotters. 'You can eat everything off a pig.'

Pete. The Dad. Short, elf-like face, false teeth too big for his mouth, beaming out a fixed, slightly unsettling smile, rarely uttering a word, always wearing a paisley cap, even indoors. He rode a bike everywhere, wobbling in the middle of the road on his way home from the pub, occasionally falling off it, finishing up under a hedge or on a front lawn, a phone call to Doreen who'd get one of the boys to go and fetch him home.

Ryan. The youngest brother. Body builder, sweat vest, eagle tattoo on the bicep of his right arm, dealt in scrap metal, a wad of cash held together with an elastic band in his back pocket, peeling off notes like a croupier dealing cards in a game of pontoon, most of his adult life spent with Social Security on his case, father unknown written on the birth certificates of his three kids.

Stuart. The middle one. A red eye patch covering his left eye, someone fired a pellet into it when he was a kid, making him a nightmare driver, throwing his pick-up around corners, drifting over to the wrong side of the road or up the kerb. He laughs at everything – inappropriate affect the doctors called it – and can't sit still, up and down to the window. 'For Christ's sake sit down, Stu,' snapped Lorraine.

Doreen looked over her glasses at me, pausing as if trying to remember something. 'Freddie,' she said, looking relieved. 'Is your mum not coming?'

'Not tonight. '

She smiled and went back to looking at the baby.

'I saw Keith in the pub last night,' said Ryan.

'Ryan,' said Lorraine, pulling the baby closer to her and nodding at me.

'He doesn't mind. Do you, mate?'

'Of course not. Why should I?'

'Have you thought of a name?' said Doreen.

'I can't decide,' said Lorraine.

'Becky,' said Pete.

We all looked at him.

'Nice name, Becky,' he said.


*Freddie's Book*

---

God walked back to the hand-cart. 'Shall we see what's underneath?'

'Soul mates; Soul mates; Soul mates'

With a single stroke he whipped the tarpaulin aside.

The crowd gasped.

'Behold, my people. The hideous original human.'

Shackled to the cart by an ironmongery of thick chain was a two headed Humpty Dumpty creature with four arms and four legs, its faces covered with bolted on iron clown masks. No sound emerged from either head, but all four arms reached out in pleading fashion to the crowd.

'See how it begs for forgiveness.'

God held his hands aloft and walked to the edge of the stage.

'And so it should. I gave them everything, gave them a powerful life, and they betrayed me, threatened to usurp the gods.'

The crowd booed.

'But they paid a price,' said God, pointing at Chardonnay, who was still frozen like an ice sculpture in the arbitration room below. 'Cut in half, I damned them to spend all eternity searching for their mate, their soul mate.'

A roar of laughter rang out.

I'd attended a care conference in Leeds and had booked to stay in one of the local bed and breakfast places five minutes' walk away from the university campus. I always hoped Lorraine would try and persuade me to drive home from these things, say Becky would miss me, but she never did. 'You should stay. Get to know people. Widen your networks.' She was right. She was always right.

I should have called, shouldn't have popped up out of the blue, disrupting her plans, but I wanted to surprise her and the last session had been cancelled. 'You're too predictable, Freddie. I know everything you're thinking and doing.' She would never have expected me to drive home, not without calling first.

I pulled into the driveway, pulled up behind Lorraine's yellow Mini, which meant she was in, but there were no lights on in the house and all the curtains were drawn. The curtains didn't bother me, but no lights was unusual. Perhaps she'd gone to bed, had one of her migraines. I told myself to be careful, not to wake her, not to wake Becky.

I eased out of the car, crunched my way as softly as I could up the gravel driveway, put my key in the lock, opened the front door and stepped into the house, gently closing the door behind me. I heard the toilet flush, which made me look up the stairs at the bathroom door directly in front of me. The door opened and Keith appeared, wearing nothing but boxer shorts. He looked straight at me. 'Lorraine,' he said. 'Lover boy's back.'

She'd been seeing him for months, taking Becky to stay at her parents. I think she was relieved when I found out. She appeared next to him, still pulling on her dressing gown.

'Freddie,' she said. 'You should have called.'

The cul-de-sac had changed since Mum's time. Neighbours who'd lived in their houses for years had moved into the new sheltered housing scheme three streets away, with its on-site bistro and gym facilities. Either that or they'd died, leaving their three-bedroom detached houses to young families with unaffordable mortgages and uncontrollable kids.

I imagined what's wrong with him rumours doing the rounds at meal-tables – a man, living alone with four cats, the kids listening, taking it all in. Not right is it? Who chooses to live like that? Have you seen him locking his front door? I stopped reacting when the kids knocked the door and ran away, or when they peered through the lounge window, or when they kicked their football against my house wall. Reacting only fuelled it, rewarded their behaviour, acted as encouragement. I didn't want them hurting the cats. Best to keep my head down, get in the house as quickly as possible. Keep the cats in as much as I could.

*Freddie's Book*

Chardonnay sniffed in the sweet scented apple orchard of the afterlife. She'd read somewhere that nothing ever truly starts or ends. The end of one thing must by definition be the start of something new. She'd died, she remembered dying, but she was still here, seeing, smelling, touching; thinking about the future, pondering the consequences of her death, wondering what would happen next. Heaven. Hell. Plato's souls racing out of the shadows at Olympic sprinter speed back to the perfect cave. Buddhism's infinite cycle of re-birth until Nirvana. It all boiled down to the same thing. Death wasn't the end. It was a new beginning and that meant she could find him, be with him again.

'I'm coming, my darling,' she whispered. 'I'm coming.'

## Jo-Jo – July 2015

Jason used to enjoy his candy time. That's what he called it. Candy time. 'You mean you want to screw me.'

'Don't say that.'

'Why not? It's what you want to do.' Screw was exactly what it was. Him grunting through ten minutes of exertion, racing to his climax, falling on top of me, rolling off me like I was radioactive, no kissing, no tenderness, no cuddling, walking the few steps back to his bed, facing the wall, asking me if I'd come as an afterthought. 'Yes. Thank you.' That annoyed him. Me thanking him in the same voice I used when he'd done the washing up. I'd wipe him away in the toilet, flush him down the drain, go back into the bedroom, put the light on and change the sheet. 'Do you have to do that now?'

And then I'd lie there, listening to his snoring, trying to imagine what Mum's life had been like. Schizophrenia, split mind, shattered thoughts, disembodied voices. 'I talk back to them, Jo-Jo. They're like my friends.'

'They're not real, Mum.'

'Of course they are, sweetheart.' The tranquilisers numbed her, sucked her away; turned her into a zombie.

I used to talk to myself, say it'll get better, having a child was going to make it all okay, give me a purpose.

Freddie and I were still sitting on the hotel's garden bench.

'Why didn't you phone me, Freddie?'

'When?'

'When I went to university. You said you'd call, wait for me, and then you didn't.'

He let go of my hand and looked at the ground.

'I thought that's what you wanted. To get on with your new life. It was for the best, Jo-Jo.'

'The best?'

'That's what I thought. Like I said, you were way out of my league.'

'But not to call, not to say goodbye. That was cruel. You just left me.'

'You could have called me,' he said.

'It wasn't that simple. It got complicated.'

'I was going to call when your dad died, but I didn't think you'd want me to.'

'You're right, by then it was too late, but at the beginning… when it really mattered…'

I could feel the adrenaline pumping through my veins, hear my heartbeat in my head. I didn't want to have this conversation. My plan was to see him one last time, make sure he was okay, bury the demons, say goodbye. Closure. Not this. I didn't want to talk about this.

I stood up and walked away from the bench.

'Jo-Jo,' he called.

I stopped walking.

He came to my side. I was crying.

'I'm sorry,' he said. 'But I didn't think you wanted me. I never thought I was good enough for you. If I'd have known.'

'I needed you so much, Freddie.'

He gently lifted my chin and looked into my eyes. 'I love you, Jo-Jo. I've always loved you. Please don't go.'

I touched him on the cheek. 'It's too late, Freddie. We were so good, you and I, but you should have called.'

I walked out of the garden.

I used to watch my neighbours opposite occupy their white plastic chair. It was positioned underneath the carport, next to the electric box, placed in-between a grey rubbish bin and a small patio table, which someone, years ago, has sprayed green. The table held an ashtray or a coffee mug or a can of lager or a newspaper, depending on who was occupying the chair; the spray paint was flaking, showing up patches of a coppery metallic base. If a group or a pair of people gathered under the carport, the chair stayed empty. Sitting down meant you were on your own. That was the rule.

The thinker. She spent a lot of time in the chair, out there in all weathers, five thirty in the morning, the middle of December, frost on the cars, head bowed, huddled in her paisley pyjamas, drawing hard through pursued lips on a filter free cigarette, smoky breath vaporising in the chilly air, occasionally lifting her head and surveying the street. I called her Gertie – the game was more fun with a name. It suited her. I was behind her once in the local shop. 'Give us a pack of me smokes, love.' Nicotine stained fingers and teeth, deep ravine wrinkles running across her forehead, strips of flabby skin hanging from her neck. Goose neck my mum called it. Gertie didn't live in the house. She was an Aunt who looked after the kids once a month, letting them go away for long weekends. She looked like she'd lived a life. That's what she must have been thinking about.

I didn't look back to see if Freddie was following me. I ran up the steps to the hotel entrance and, forcing myself to stop running, walked through the doors into the lobby. The receptionist lifted his head in greeting and then dropped a concerned look on his face when he saw me.

'Are you okay, madam?'

'I'm fine,' I said, without looking at him. 'Just in a hurry.'

I turned back towards the entrance doors, half expecting to see Freddie walking up the steps, coming to find me. I looked across the car park and spotted him walking towards Jack's Mini with his head bowed, hands in his pockets. He got in the car, started the engine and drove away down the tree lined hotel exit route.

'Mum.'

Amy was at my side.

'I thought you'd gone for a walk,' I said.

'I changed my mind. I've been waiting for you in the conservatory. Have you been crying? Where is he?'

'He's gone, sweetheart.'

'Gone? What did he say?'

'That he loved me. That he'd always loved me.'

'And?'

'He doesn't want me to go. He wants me to be part of his life.'

She threw her arms around me. 'Oh Mum, that's great. And don't worry about New Zealand. We'll sort that out. Maybe you can rent somewhere here for six months or a year. See how it goes with this Freddie. I'll call the estate agents.' She was rubbing my back. I could smell her leather jacket.

'You don't understand, Amy. I need to come with you.'


*Freddie – July 2015*

---

Back at my kitchen table, I looked again at the picture of me and Jo-Jo.

Maybe I should have followed her into the hotel, told her about my going to Lincoln, seeing her with the bowler hat man, but all I could think about was that I'd made her cry. What was the point of raking over old ashes? We'd both had lives. She'd been married, had a family. If I could turn the clock back I'd call, help her settle in, wait for her, but, at the time, it felt right. She was moving into a new circle, a circle that I didn't and could never fit. And now she was moving on again, emigrating.

Another photo dropped into my head. A two-year-old girl. Her hair in pigtails, wearing a white dress with a navy blue trim, black leather buckled shoes and short white socks that were pinching her legs. She was smiling. Forty minutes it had taken us to get that smile – forty minutes of treading on eggshells, pulling faces and waving her teddy bear. Three years later she was gone, out of my life, a new dad, a new city.

I shook my head and turned the packet of beta-blockers over and over in my hand. The kitchen walls were closing in on me. A feeling of nausea dropped into my stomach like a lead weight.

A memory. I look in the rear view mirror. There's a flash of light. It could have been the sun. I flick the indicator to turn right. 'What are you doing?'

'Turning round. I need to check something.'

'Not this again, Freddie. Becky needs her tea.' I drive back towards the speed camera. There's another one on this side of the road, trapping me in both directions. I check the speedometer. Thirty miles an hour. I feel pressure on my right foot. I want to press harder. Go faster. Go faster. 'Can we go home now?' she says, looking at Becky asleep on the back seat. I turn the car around and drive back towards the first camera. The pressure's back on my foot. Another flash of light. It is the sun. Thank God.

It wasn't about thirty-five years ago. It was about now. When I'd said I loved her, didn't want her to go, that's when she'd got

136

upset. Panicked. Didn't know what to say. All she'd wanted was to say goodbye and I'd made it complicated. She'd needed an escape route. That was it.

I dropped my head on the kitchen table and sobbed.


*Jo-Jo – July 2015*

---

Amy put her arm around me and walked me quickly across the hotel lobby, up the stairs and into my bedroom. She shot the receptionist a glare as we walked by. He lowered his head and went back to looking at his computer screen. 'It'll be okay, Mum,' she was whispering over and over as we walked. I was holding a balled up tissue that I'd found in my handbag. I could feel my head filling up with fluid, ready to gush out if I lost my 'I don't want to cry' concentration. It crossed my mind that Amy was embarrassed, trying to get me out of sight. Her mother having a breakdown in public was not a good look. That was unfair.

We reached my room. She sat me gently on the bed, walked over to the mini-bar fridge and pulled out two miniature bottles of Jack Daniels. She blew the dust out of two tumblers, like they do in the cowboy movies, poured a full bottle of whiskey into each glass and thrust one in my hand.

'Drink it,' she said.

'I don't like whiskey.'

She put her hand under my glass and nudged it gently towards my mouth. 'It's medicinal, Mum.'

I took a sip of the Jack Daniels and swallowed, wincing a little as it burned the back of my throat.

She nudged the glass again. 'And another.'

I did as I was told, this time taking more of a slurp than a sip. Amy did the same.

'He seems nice, Mum. I think he still loves you.'

'I know, darling. I know.'

She hugged me close. 'One day you're going to tell me the full story. We'll sit in the garden and work our way through a bottle of New Zealand Chardonnay.'

'I'd like that,' I said. 'I'd like that very much.'

*Freddie – July 2015*

---

I walked to the station, my head bowed, hugging into my leather jacket; my eyes on the pavement. It was drizzling with rain and the wind was getting up. I quickened my pace. A couple walked past me, but all I saw were their shoes. A bus sloshed by, workmen were drilling the road, surrounded by bollards. I reached the station, walked past the ticket operator, looked up at the departures board and looked at my watch.

I headed for the platform.

'Nasty day,' said an old man huddled on one of the wooden benches. I smiled, but said nothing. He scowled at me, muttered 'Manners,' and went back to his book.

The train came into view.

I removed my Ray-ban spectacles and put them in my coat pocket.

I stared at the track for a few seconds and then looked again at the old man.

'Freddie.'

I looked in the direction of the voice. It was Jack. He was running towards me.

I looked again at the train. It had nearly reached me.

'Freddie,' Jack called again.

# ABOUT THE AUTHOR

Photograph by TC

Stephen Brotherton lives in Telford and is a Social Worker. Another Shot is his first novel.